ADIRONDACK MOUSE

AND

THE MYSTERIOUS DISAPPEARANCE

OTHER BOOKS BY IRENE UTTENDORFSKY

CHAPTER BOOKS FOR YOUNG READERS

Adirondack Mouse and the Perilous Journey, <u>Adirondack Center for Writing Literary Award: 2006 Best Children's Book.</u>

HISTORICAL FICTION

A Punkeyville Girl: A Tale of Old Forestport and the Canals

Hannah and the Two Sisters: An Erie Canal Adventure

When Thunder Rolls: The Underground Railroad and the Civil War

ADIRONDACK MOUSE
AND
THE MYSTERIOUS DISAPPEARANCE

BY

IRENE UTTENDORFSKY

ILLUSTRATIONS

BY

ALLEN A. KRAEGER

SPRUCE GULCH PRESS

BOX 4347

ROME, NY

13442

Published by Spruce Gulch Press
Rome, NY 13442

Graphic support
by
Graphics of Utica

Printed by Graphics of Utica

ISBN   978-0-984 1259 - 0-6

For Dorothy & Sammy

ACKNOWLEDGEMENTS

I am indebted to Random House Children's Books, a division of Random House, Inc., for their permission to use the cover of their book, ONE FISH, TWO FISH, RED FISH, BLUE FISH, by Dr. Seuss, as an illustration in this book and for permission to use the name of the book in my story; to Katie Noonan, Marketing Director, The Enchanted Forest/ Water Safari, Old Forge, NY; for permission to use a photo of The Enchanted Forest/Water Safari in an illustration; to Allen A. Kraeger for bringing my story to life with his magical drawings; to Elaine, owner, Graphics of Utica, for bringing together picture and photograph, transforming illustrations from vision to reality; to my daughter Susan, for her editing expertise; to Isabella Worthen, Director, Old Forge Library and Hope Marston, Author, for their thoughtful reviews; to Sandy, Ryan, Melissa and Levi for their helpful comments; to my husband for his useful critiques and for just putting up with me; to Patricia Langendorf, Owner, Spruce Gulch Press, for believing in me and Adirondack Mouse.

TABLE OF CONTENTS

CHAPTER 1

AND THE WINNER IS . . .

Adirondack Mouse waved his paw and shouted, "Hello!" to the other young mice. All the clans of the North Country Field Mice had come together again along the side of Park Hill to celebrate the harvest at the Gathering. Like Adirondack, many wore the orange scarf of the Pumpkin Clan. Other mice wore the red scarf of the Apple Clan. And still others wore the purple scarf of the Grape Clan.

"Adirondack!" one of the mice shouted. "Hey, it's Adirondack, back from his Journey!" They all ran to catch up with him.

"I can't stop to talk right now," Adirondack said. "I'm looking for Melvin. Have you seen him?"

"I saw him," the smallest mouse said. "He was on his way to the starting line for the Cider Blaster Race."

"Thanks," Adirondack said. "That's where I thought I would find him."

He jogged toward the starting line. He wanted to get there before the race started so he could wish Melvin luck.

1

Then he would cheer Melvin on, all the way to the finish line. Melvin was sure to win, just like he did last year.

Adirondack sniffed the air. He smelled smoke from the cooking fires. He smelled hot, cinnamon-y apple pie. He smelled tart blueberry pudding. And best of all he smelled his favorite, sugary baked pumpkin.

His tummy growled, but Adirondack didn't stop for even one quick bite. There would be plenty of time to sample the feast after he found Melvin. Everything always tasted better when you shared it with your friend.

By the time Adirondack reached the starting line the race had begun. The runners were out of sight and the mice who had come to cheer for their friends had moved on toward the finish line.

Adirondack panted as he ran down the short cut path to the finish line. This will be even better, he thought. He imagined Melvin's look of surprise when he crossed the finish line and saw Adirondack standing there.

When Adirondack got to the end of the track, he elbowed his way through the crowd of mice until he stood behind the finish line. He looked down the track. Melvin should be coming any minute now.

I can hardly wait to tell Melvin about my Journey, Adirondack thought. He'll understand how scared I was when that cat almost caught me. And he'll know what a shock it was to wake up and find a huge snake tickling my toes. I can't wait to tell him all about my new friend, Kate, and my trip to the Adirondack Mountains.

I think that's the most wonderful part about a best friend. You can tell him anything and he never makes fun of you. Not even behind your back. And he won't tell anybody else if you ask him not to.

Adirondack heard paws running toward the finish line. He couldn't see who it was, but it had to be Melvin.

"Way to go, Melvin!" he shouted, waving his scarf and jumping up and down.

The other mice took up the cheer. "Melvin! Melvin! Melvin!" they chanted.

"Here he comes!" someone shouted.

All the mice yelled, "Hurrah!"

Melvin must be tired, Adirondack thought. He should have come around the curve by now.

Finally the winning racer came around the bend. Adirondack dropped his scarf. His eyes bugged out.

The crowd stopped cheering. They looked. They blinked. They looked again, as if they couldn't believe their eyes.

CHAPTER 2

THE MYSTERIOUS DISAPPEARANCE

"Get out of my way, Pipsqueak!" Rupert yelled as he stumbled across the finish line.

Adirondack backed off the track.

"I won!" Rupert shouted. "Where's my crown of grape leaves, you losers?"

The crowd stared. No one cheered.

The mayor of Seed Hollow stepped forward. "Ahem," he said. "As Mayor of the great and glorious Village of Seed Hollow, I crown you winner of this year's Cider Blaster." He looked very unhappy when he placed the circle of green leaves on Rupert's head.

Adirondack couldn't believe this. Rupert had never run a race in his whole life! And he wasn't even out of breath.

"Look at me," Rupert said. "I'm king of the stupid Cider Blaster! When I tell the storyteller that I won this dumb race, he'll have to choose me to be the next storyteller."

"Where's Melvin?" Adirondack asked.

"What's that?" Rupert said. He looked at Adirondack for the first time. His eyes got bigger as he realized who he was looking at.

"Don't tell me the crybaby came back," Rupert said. He laughed his mean laugh and pointed at Adirondack. "Look everybody. Look what the cat hawked up."

"Where is Melvin?" Adirondack asked again.

"Awww," Rupert said. "Poor little Adirondack. By the time he crawled out of the cat's belly he couldn't find his little friend. Too bad, too. I wanted Melvin to be the one to carry me back to the Gathering. But he's probably hiding somewhere, crying his eyes out because I won and he lost."

"Melvin can run faster than you," Adirondack said. "He should have won."

"Ha, ha, ha," Rupert laughed. "Don't pay any attention to this loser," he said to the mayor. "Now who's going to carry me to the celebration?"

Adirondack sighed. All the mice looked unhappy. They looked a little scared too. Who could blame them? Rupert was one mean mouse!

Rupert stomped his foot.

Two mice stepped forward. They groaned as they lifted Rupert up on their shoulders.

"Giddy-up," Rupert shouted, like he was riding on a couple of meadow moles. "Last one at the party is a big old stinkbug!"

Adirondack waited until they were all out of sight. Where is Melvin, he wondered. There is no way he would have missed entering this race. So why didn't he win?

Adirondack walked up the race track. Maybe Melvin fell and hurt himself, he thought. Maybe he needs help.

He walked faster. He looked from one side of the track to the other. But he didn't see any sign of his friend.

He kept walking, farther and farther up the track. All of a sudden he saw something caught in a tree up ahead. When he got closer he saw a small piece of blue cloth hanging from a low branch of a pine tree. The cloth waved in the breeze, as if it wanted to make sure he saw it.

"This might be a clue," Adirondack said. He reached for the cloth, but he couldn't reach it. He stood on tiptoes and tried again. No luck. Then he took a running start and jumped as high as he could.

"Hooray!" he shouted as he grabbed the prize and pulled it off the limb. He tumbled down to the ground still hanging onto the cloth.

Adirondack got up and brushed the dry pine needles off his jacket. He held the scrap of cloth between his front paws. The cloth felt soft and silky. When he turned the cloth over, Adirondack couldn't believe his eyes. On the other side of that cloth, written in white, was the number 1! The number worn by the winner of last year's race. The number Melvin should have been wearing.

Adirondack studied the scrap of cloth. "It is a clue," he said. "But what does it mean?" He thought and thought. "Well, if this is the number that was on Melvin's shirt, somebody or something must have ripped it off." He frowned. "I think I need to look for more clues." He tucked the cloth into his knapsack and started walking again.

A little farther down the track Adirondack stubbed his paw on a small rock. "Ow!" he yelled. He hopped up and down on three paws until the one that hurt felt better. Then he looked around.

The fallen leaves that should have covered the rock had been scattered around. When he got down on his knees, the ground looked like somebody or something had fallen and rolled around on it.

"Maybe I'll find another clue here," he said. He followed the trail of messed up leaves to the very edge of the track. Beyond the track the ground went down a steep hill. Adirondack looked down the hill. The leaves had been pushed away in one wide stripe, like somebody or something had slid down that hill.

Melvin? If it was Melvin he might still be down there.

"I'm coming, Melvin," Adirondack yelled.

CHAPTER 3

BLOO

Adirondack found a sturdy grape vine growing near the edge of the race track. He held on to the vine and started down the hill backwards. Paw-over-paw, with his hind paws pushing off against the side of the hill, he slowly made his way down to the ground below. Just like a man in the picture he had seen in one of Kate's school books. She said it was a picture of a famous mountain climber.

"Wow," Adirondack said. "I'm a mountain climber, too."

When he reached the flat ground at the bottom of the hill he let go of the vine.

"Spro-i-ng," said the vine. And then, "Whoosh," as it snapped back up to the top of the hill. Adirondack looked up. The hill was very steep. And the vine that he could have used to climb back up waved to him from the very top.

"I wish I had kept that vine down here with me," Adirondack said. "It will take me a long time to get back up the hill without it."

Wherever he looked here at the bottom of the hill he saw trees. Dark green evergreen trees and tall maple trees with red and yellow leaves. Some of the pretty leaves floated down to the ground as he watched. Dry leaves covered most of the ground as thick as a rug, except for the spot where Adirondack stood. Here it looked like someone or something had brushed all the leaves away.

"Squawk!"

Adirondack looked up. Blue Jay hopped up and down on a branch above his head.

"Blue Jay!" Adirondack said. "I'm so glad to see you. Have you seen another mouse around here? I'm looking for my friend, Melvin."

"Squawk!" Blue Jay said. "I was just sunning myself on that rock over there when a hawk came after me. I flew away and hid in a big pine tree until he was gone. If there was a mouse around here I didn't see him. If you ask me, he's probably hiding, too."

Adirondack sat down on a toadstool. "I have to find my friend Melvin," he said. "He may need my help." He looked up at Blue Jay. "Can you help me look for a clue?"

"Squawk?" Blue Jay said. "What's a clue?"

"A clue is something we can use to help us find Melvin," Adirondack said. "It might be a broken branch or a line of small stones. It might just be something that looks different."

Adirondack jumped up and pointed to the ground near his feet. "Look at how these leaves have been moved off this spot. That could be a clue!"

"Well," Blue Jay said. He ruffled his feathers and cocked his head to one side. "I was looking at those strange marks in the dirt over there before you got here."

"What marks?" Adirondack said. He stepped back and studied the bare ground. "Oh," he said. "Yes! I see."

He kneeled down and traced the marks with his paw:

BLOO

CHAPTER 4

WHAT ABOUT MELVIN?

"What do you think that means?" Blue Jay asked. "I don't know," Adirondack said. "But it has to be a clue." He pulled a pencil and scrap of paper out of his knapsack. He carefully copied the marks onto his paper and then tucked the paper back inside his knapsack.

When he finished, he looked up at the sun through the tree tops. "It's getting late," he said. "I'd better start back up the hill."

"Did you happen to see any sunflower seeds up there?" Blue Jay asked.

Adirondack smiled. "No, but we field mice are having our Gathering there."

"Oh," Blue Jay said. He looked bored.

"The Gathering is the finest fair you ever saw," Adirondack said. "Even better than the Boonville Fair that my friend Kate took me to last summer. Except for the Ferris Wheel. Sitting at the top of that huge wheel was the coolest thing I have ever done."

"Right," Blue Jay said. "But I can fly higher than that."

"Well, they also have lots of good things to eat at the Gathering," Adirondack said. "I think you'd like the sugary baked pumpkin."

"Squawk!" Blue Jay said. "Hop on my back. I'll give you a ride up the hill if you will find me some of that pumpkin."

"Be careful," Adirondack said. "I've only done this once before." He climbed up and sat close to Blue Jay's head so he could hang on with both paws.

Blue Jay flew straight up in the air. The wind from his wings blew Adirondack's ears straight back and made him squint his eyes. Just when he thought he couldn't hang onto Blue Jay's neck one more minute, they stopped climbing and floated off on an unseen river of air.

Adirondack opened his eyes and looked down at a fluffy white cloud. Down? At a cloud? He hugged Blue Jay's neck tighter and closed his eyes again. "Take me back!" he shouted. "Why did you fly so high?"

"So you could show me where to land," Blue Jay said. "When we reach that break in the clouds over there," he said dipping one wing to point –

"Don't do that," Adirondack yelled. "I'll fall off."

"Look," Blue Jay said.

Adirondack opened his eyes. They had sailed through the opening in the clouds and floated high above Park Hill. Tiny wisps of smoke twirled up from the campfires.

13

"You have to fly down closer," Adirondack said. "I can't see where to land from way up here."

"But if I leave this stream of air I will either have to fly away or land," Blue Jay said. He flapped his wings once and they sailed ahead. "What is that delicious smell?"

Adirondack sniffed the air. "That's it!" he shouted. "That's sugary baked pumpkin."

"Sugary baked pumpkin here I come!" Blue Jay yelled. He rolled into a steep dive.

Adirondack closed his eyes and held his breath. The wind clawed at him, trying to tear him off the bird's back. He gritted his teeth and held on tighter. Finally Blue Jay pulled out of his dive, and lightly touched the ground as he landed right next to the food tents.

Adirondack picked stray feathers out of his teeth before he hopped down.

The baker mouse backed into his tent. He peeked out from behind the door flap.

"Squawk!" Blue Jay said.

The baker mouse swayed. He wobbled, like he was about to fall down.

Adirondack ran into the tent. "Please sir," he said. "Can I have a piece of your sugary baked pumpkin for my friend?"

"Take as much as you want," the baker said. He stared at Blue Jay with round eyes.

Adirondack scooped up five big pieces. "You have to promise me you won't beg for more," he said as he gave them to Blue Jay.

"Mmmmm!" Blue Jay said. "Tasty and sweet." He swallowed every piece and then hopped up and down. He cocked his head and winked his eye. "Is it all right if I fly up in that tree and wait for somebody to drop a crumb or two?" he asked.

Adirondack laughed. "You're hopeless," he said. "All you ever think about is your stomach. Just don't scare the baker again," he added as he walked away.

He headed for his mom and dad's tent. He had to tell them about Melvin's disappearance. But when he saw the storyteller's tent and his walking stick leaning against the flap, he forgot all about that.

In three days the storyteller will choose somebody to be the next storyteller, Adirondack said to himself. I've waited a whole year for that. If I tell the storyteller everything that happened to me on my perilous Journey he is sure to choose me.

But what about Melvin? What if no one finds him? What if something grabbed him and took him far away? Will the elders just say, 'a hawk must have got him,' like they did when my dad disappeared? And then just forget about him?

"Not if I have anything to say about it," Adirondack said to an inchworm on a maple leaf. The inchworm stretched himself out straight and then pulled his tail back up to his head. He didn't even look at Adirondack; he just carefully measured another inch of the leaf.

"But if I go away to look for Melvin I might not get back in time for the storytelling. And if I'm not here the storyteller will choose another mouse. And that mouse will be the storyteller for all of the North Country Field Mice until he's too old to remember the stories anymore. By then, I'll be too old, too. I'll never have another chance to be storyteller in my whole life."

But what about Melvin?

CHAPTER 5

ADIRONDACK MAKES A CHOICE

Adirondack jingled the silver bell that hung beside the flap on the storyteller's tent.

"Who's there?" The storyteller poked his head out. "Why it's Adirondack!" he cried. The wrinkles on his face disappeared as his mouth curved into a smile. "I didn't know you had come back from your perilous Journey. Come in, come in. I can't wait to hear your stories."

Adirondack stepped inside the storyteller's tent. A table made of willow branches stood in the middle of the tent. Small twigs threaded under and over one another formed the lacy table top. A huge book with a red velvet cover lay open on the table. Adirondack made a bee-line for that book.

He had never seen a mouse-size book before. It looked a lot like the big books he had seen at the Adirondack School. But when he looked closer at the open page, it didn't look anything like the pages in the People's school books. Line after line of marks and signs covered each page.

Drawings of pictures sprinkled here and there between the lines and around the edges. He traced the marks with his paw.

"This book tells the history of the North Country field mice," the storyteller said. "Every story that has been told since the first two field mice came together in peace is written here."

"Wow!" Adirondack said. "I didn't know anyone knew how to write them down. I didn't know anyone could read either."

The storyteller chuckled. "That's the real work of the storyteller. Do you think anyone could remember all those stories? It's my job to write down every story I hear during my lifetime. They are all part of our history, you know. How we live, what we say, what makes us laugh, what makes us cry; that's our history. We each make our own stories as we go through life."

"That's true," Adirondack said. "But only one mouse knows how to write them down and save them for all the mice who will come after him. That makes the storyteller the most important mouse in the world, doesn't it? But how do you pick the next storyteller? How do you know who will do the best job?"

"The same way old storytellers have always made that choice. By watching and listening to the young mice as they come of age. It's easy for me to see who is honest and dependable, who can be trusted to keep the stories true.

Those are the ones I will consider. Then all I need to do is to see which one of those few can tell the best stories."

"I love to tell stories," Adirondack said softly. He patted the open page of the book. "But this must take a long time, I mean, learning to read and write. And how can you be sure you will hear and write down every story? And how do you dare to write in this wonderful book?"

"Do you like it?" the storyteller asked. He smiled. "Perhaps someday you will be the keeper of the storybook."

Adirondack whirled around. "Me? Do you think so? Do you really think so?"

The storyteller chuckled. "Well, first I'll have to hear all about your Journey, but if you can keep a secret –"

"I can't," Adirondack said. He hung his head.

"What's that?" the storyteller said. "Do you mean to say you can't keep a secret?"

"No. I mean I can't stay long enough to tell you my stories." Adirondack said. "And I may not be able to come to the storytelling." He brushed a tear from his eye. "I might not even be here when you choose the next storyteller. That's what I came to tell you."

CHAPTER 6

THE RIGHT THING TO DO

"That was the hardest thing I've ever had to do," Adirondack told his mom later. "Especially after the storyteller told me that I had a very good chance of being the one chosen."

"Maybe you should go back and tell him you've changed your mind," his mom said. "Your father has gone to tell the elders Melvin is missing. They'll search every inch of Park Hill."

"But what if they can't find him? I have a bad feeling about Melvin, Mom. I think somebody took him away from here. If the elders can't find him, I'll have to go and look for him."

"But you and your father have just come back home," his mom said. "I don't want you to go away again. Can't someone else look for Melvin?"

"He's an orphan, Mom. I'm sure if his mom and dad had survived the spring flood two seasons ago, they would try to find him. But they're gone."

"I could go," his dad said as he came into the tent. "If we don't find Melvin here I'll keep searching until I do."

Adirondack shook his head. "Your leg is still weak from our long walk home, and you will be up half the night tonight searching here. Besides, I know where to get help with the clues I've found." He held up the paper from his knapsack. "I think I've seen marks like this in Kate's school books. She can help me figure out what it means."

"But what if you never find Melvin?" his dad said. "What if something happens to you, too?" He put one paw on Adirondack's shoulder. "Are you certain you want to risk your own life and give up your only chance to be storyteller? For Melvin?"

"I don't know how anybody could ever be certain of that," Adirondack said. "But it's the right thing to do. My best friend has disappeared and he may be in great danger. If I don't do everything I can to help him, I will never forgive myself. And if I stay here and he never comes back, I'll spend the rest of my life wondering if I could have found him before it was too late."

"Then you have made the right choice, my son," his dad said.

His mom brushed a tear from her eye. "Why does it have to be you who goes?"

"Because I have the best chance of finding Melvin. I faced many dangers on my perilous Journey and I learned lots of lessons. I learned to live with some North Country

People and their cat. I traveled all the way to the Adirondack Mountains. And I rescued my friend, Kate, from Bald Mountain when she hurt her leg and couldn't walk. No other mouse in Seed Hollow has done all that."

His mom put her arms around him. "I was right to name you 'Adirondack'," she said. "You really are as strong and as brave as the mountains."

Adirondack's face reddened with pleasure. He smiled from ear to ear.

"That's true," his dad said. "Without his help I would still be trapped in a fish tank in the Adirondack School." He gave Adirondack a big hug.

"A hero like that should have a special treat before he goes off on another Journey," his mom said. She went outside to the cooking fire, and soon the tent was filled with the most wonderful smells. In no time she came back with two plates of food, one for Adirondack and one for his dad. Each plate was piled high with roasted corn sprinkled with goldenrod seed.

"Mmmmm!" Adirondack said when he took a bite. The corn tasted as sweet as candy and the crunchy goldenrod seeds burst with spicy flavor when he chewed them between his teeth.

"I sure have missed your cooking, Martha," his dad said.

"Me, too," Adirondack agreed. He ate every kernel of corn and licked up all the goldenrod seed. When he finished, he patted his tummy. Then he yawned and stretched.

"It's time you went to bed," his mom said. "Maybe your father and the other elders will find Melvin tonight."

"I hope so," Adirondack said. He kissed his mom and hopped on his bed of dried leaves. His dandelion fluff pillow felt soft as a sack of hummingbird feathers. He fell asleep at once.

Once or twice he awoke to the sound of distant voices calling, "Melvin? Melvin!" Each time, before he went back to sleep, he crossed his paws and wished that Melvin would hear them call and come out to be rescued.

Adirondack's mom shook him awake before the sun came up. "Your father just came back from the search," she said. "I'm afraid he has bad news."

CHAPTER 7

THE LEAVING

The light from his dad's firefly lantern danced all around the tent. "We looked everywhere, but we didn't find any sign of Melvin," he said. "The mayor of Seed Hollow has called off the search so I came home. He says there's nothing more we can do."

"I knew that would happen," Adirondack said. "Well, I'm not going to give up on Melvin."

"I packed your knapsack while you were sleeping," his mom said. "And I want to give you a present before you go." She handed him a package wrapped in dried grass and tied up with a piece of wood vine.

"I made it for you right after you left on your perilous Journey," she said as he tore off the wrapping. "I planned to give it to you after the storytelling. It was supposed to be a welcome home gift, not a going-away present."

"Wow!" Adirondack said as he slipped on his new bright green coat. "It fits me like a new skin fits a snake."

Mom handed him his knapsack. "Try not to lose your jacket this time. I'm hoping I won't have enough time to make another one before you return."

Adirondack laughed. "With any luck Melvin and I will be back before the storytelling begins."

His dad walked him outside. "Take the lantern so you can see your way in the dark," he said. "Just don't forget to let the fireflies out when the sun comes up."

"Thanks, Dad. I won't forget." Adirondack looked into the dark shadows. The flashing lantern light made the bushes and trees seem to jump and change shape as the fireflies blinked their lights on and off. Branches and twigs twisted and turned like monsters trying to catch hold of him. He wanted to run back to his bed and bury his head under his pillow until the sun came up. But if he wasted time waiting for the sun, he might not find Melvin in time to help him.

"I'll be back as soon as I can, Dad," Adirondack said. He held the lantern high as he walked away, and tried hard not to think about the scary night creatures that lurked beyond the light. When he turned back to wave, the dark had already swallowed up his dad and their tent.

As long as he held the lantern high, he could see well enough to keep from walking off the edge of a cliff or falling in a stream. Once he got used to the moving limbs and branches he felt less afraid.

"Who? Who, who, who?"

Owl!

Adirondack dived behind a tree and peeked around the trunk. Big yellow eyes high up in a tree searched this way and that. Adirondack took off his new jacket and used it to cover his lantern.

Please go away, he wanted to say. Melvin needs my help. And besides, if I don't keep going I'll never make it back in time for the storytelling. But there was nothing he could do except wait for the owl to leave.

By the time the owl finally flew off, the sun had awakened, stretched its rays and peeked over a big boulder near the edge of the forest.

Adirondack brushed the dried leaves off and put his jacket on. He sat down on a log and looked at the lantern. One-by-one the fireflies put out their lights as soon as they saw the sun. When the last light flicked off, Adirondack opened the lantern door. "Fly back to your homes," he said. "But come back to me when the moon awakens."

Each firefly blinked his light before he flew away. Adirondack folded the empty lantern and tucked it into his knapsack before he set off again.

He sighed as he trudged along the path, glad he had left the Gathering before the others woke up. "The last thing I need to hear this morning is Rupert bragging about winning the Cider Blaster," he said. "And I sure don't want to hear him boasting that he's going to be the next storyteller."

Adirondack kicked a stone and sent it skipping

across the grass. "I'll bet Rupert has already gone to see the storyteller. And by now he's probably busy writing the speech he'll give when he is chosen. Rupert is right about one thing. With Melvin missing and me gone away, he is sure to win!"

Adirondack walked out of the forest and into a clearing. A tall metal object spouted water that splashed down into a big saucer at the top, dribbled over the edges and trickled back down to the water in a big pond. Adirondack put down his knapsack and knelt at the edge of the pond. He lapped up a cool drink of the shining water. He dried his mouth and whiskers with one corner of his orange scarf.

Just beyond a grassy knoll he saw a familiar black path. "I can't believe how much shorter the Journey is this time," Adirondack said to an orange and black butterfly. "It was a good idea to set out from the Gathering instead of leaving from home."

The butterfly fluttered her wings and flew around Adirondack's head. She landed on his nose. Her wings waved up and down and she looked him in the eye.

Adirondack blinked. "You fly all over the place," he said. "Have you seen a mouse? One about my size?"

The butterfly's laugh sounded like the tinkling of a hundred tiny bells. "Everywhere I look I see a mouse," she said. "I can see one right now. Haven't you seen all those mice camped along the side of this hill?" She was still laughing when she fluttered away.

"That was dumb," Adirondack said. "I should have known better than to ask such a silly question. I'm sure to a butterfly all mice look exactly the same."

He picked up his knapsack and ran across the grassy hill. He stayed away from flat rocks, where snakes like to sun themselves and cats love to nap. He looked from side to side every few minutes to be sure he didn't miss any cats sneaking up on him.

He ran down into a ditch and up the other side. He stopped at the edge of the path. With his paw above his eyes to block the bright sunlight he looked both ways. No dragons in sight. Kate would have laughed at him for calling those huge roaring things dragons. She said they were called cars. Even though he had gone for a ride in one of them with Kate and her family, he still thought they looked a lot like dragons.

Suddenly a big red dragon, breathing smoke from a silver pipe at its side, roared toward him.

I'll be safe as long as I stay off the path, he told himself. But it took all his courage not to jump into the ditch and hide. Still, he lifted his chin and stayed put even when the dragon blasted him with an ear-splitting horn. He stood there and let the wind from the dragon's breath blow his ears and whiskers straight back from his head. And he didn't move when the smoke that came out of the dragon's backside stung his eyes and his nose so bad it made him cough.

"Whew," Adirondack said after the dragon roared away. "That was the biggest one I've ever seen."

The path was empty now. He ran across to the other side and hurried through the tall grass until he reached the village sidewalk.

Several North Country People walked along the sidewalk. They seemed to be in a hurry. They chattered to each other, sometimes laughing, sometimes shouting, "Hello!" to other People they saw.

Adirondack didn't know what to do. He looked up at the sky. Where's Blue Jay when I need him? he wondered. Probably still stuffing himself full of sugary baked pumpkin! He frowned. If Blue Jay were here he could fly me to Kate's house in no time. But he's not here so I'll have to follow the sidewalk all the way to her house.

Adirondack darted into the short grass that grew beside the sidewalk. If he kept to the grass, away from the People's feet and out of their sight, this might work. He dashed from tree to tree along the sidewalk. No one even noticed. This was too easy.

All of a sudden one of the People stepped off the sidewalk to make room for another one coming from the other direction. Adirondack jumped just in time to avoid being crushed by the bottom of a huge shoe.

"Eeek! A mouse!" a lady shouted.

"Where?"

All the People stopped and stared at Adirondack. A man took off his shoe and held it up like a hammer.

Adirondack shook like a leaf in a windstorm.

CHAPTER 8

DOUBLE TROUBLE

The man with the shoe stepped closer. "I'll get him," he said.

Adirondack's heart beat like a drum. If I don't do something fast, I'm a goner, he told himself. Think! There has to be some way out of this mess.

"Hurry up!" a lady standing next to him yelled. "You know I'm scared of mice."

Adirondack looked up. The lady was dressed in short pants. She looked as pale as a fair weather cloud. She stared at Adirondack and trembled.

She's afraid of me, he thought. She's scared silly. He would have laughed out loud if the man with the shoe wasn't headed his way. Instead, he did the only thing he could. He skittered up the lady's bare leg.

"E-e-e-e-e-e-e-e-e-e!" she screamed.

Adirondack hit the ground running. No one paid any more attention to him.

The man dropped his shoe and ran to the lady. "Are you all right?" he said.

Adirondack didn't hang around to hear her answer. He raced up the main street of the village. By the time he reached Schuyler Street he had to stop to catch his breath. He hid behind a tree and peeked out at the little park with the green and white bandstand. He half expected to see Kate sitting there on the bench, reading a book. But she wasn't in the park.

He hurried on past the stop light after waiting for it to turn from red to green before he crossed the street, just like Kate had taught him to do.

Once, when he was almost at her house, he thought he heard a noise behind him. He turned around. There was nothing there but he could swear he saw a bush near the sidewalk wiggle.

Could that be a cat? He took off running and didn't stop until he stood on the porch of Kate's house. He knocked on the door as hard as he could. "Kate! It's me," he shouted. "Open the door!"

But the door didn't open.

What if she's not home? She could be in school. Or maybe she went away on vacation with her mom and dad. Or maybe she doesn't even live here anymore.

He looked over his shoulder. Something rustled in the grass near the steps. Adirondack pounded the door so hard his paws hurt. "Please!" he yelled. "Let me in!"

CHAPTER 9

KATE

The door swung open. "Adirondack!" Kate cried.

Adirondack tripped over the doorstep and fell flat on the floor inside. He scrambled to his feet. "Kate," he said. "I've never been more happy to see you in my whole life."

"What's wrong?" Kate said. She peered out the door. "Is something after you?"

"I think so," Adirondack said. "And if you don't shut that door it will get me for sure."

Kate pushed the door shut. "I hope that's not Sammy up to his old tricks. He's out there somewhere, hunting."

"Well, if he's still out there when I leave can I borrow your bell so I can ring it if he comes after me? Sammy hates that bell."

Kate laughed. "You're right about that," she said. She bent down and picked him up. "I love your new jacket. It looks cool with your orange scarf."

Adirondack felt his face redden. "My mom made it for me," he said.

Kate smiled. "I'm so glad to see you, but what brings you to our village?"

"Oh, I almost forgot," Adirondack said. "I'm looking for my friend, Melvin. He disappeared yesterday, and I was hoping you could help me figure out a clue I found."

Kate sat down on a chair at the dining room table and set Adirondack on the table top. "Show me the clue," she said.

Adirondack pulled the piece of wrinkled paper out of his knapsack. "When I went looking for Melvin I saw signs of a struggle along the side of the race track where he should have been running. I also found a piece of his running shirt with his racing number on it, so I know he was there. I followed the trail down a steep hill. At the bottom of the hill the tracks ended. That's where I discovered something written in the dirt."

He smoothed the wrinkles from his paper and put it on the table in front of Kate. "I copied the marks onto this paper. Can you tell me what they mean?"

"B-l-o-o," Kate said, spelling out each letter. "Bloo," she said out loud. She raised her eyebrows. "Bloo!" she shouted. "It sounds like our word 'blue.' Blue is a color. The color of the sky on a summer day." She laughed. "The color of Sammy's eyes."

"Blue," Adirondack said, rubbing his chin. "I don't see how that helps. Does it mean that Melvin went up in the sky? Or that a cat with blue eyes asked him to dinner?" He shook his head. "That's not much of a clue."

"Wait a minute," Kate said. "If a hawk grabbed him and took him up in the sky would he have had time to write a clue?"

"No," Adirondack said.

"And if Sammy or some other blue- eyed cat pounced on him and ate him up, would he have had time to write a clue?"

"I don't think so," Adirondack said. "But what else can it mean? Is there some place named Blue around here?"

"That's it!" Kate yelled. "Wait here, I'll get my dad's map."

A few minutes later Kate spread the map out on the dining room table. She crossed out 'BLOO' on Adirondack's paper and wrote Blue in its place. "Look for this word on the top half of the map," she said. "I'll look for it on the bottom half."

Adirondack scampered back and forth across the map. He searched for the word Blue as he ran. "There isn't much on this map," he said. "Mostly just green ground and lots of what looks like blue water."

"This is a map of the Adirondack Park," Kate said. "A lot of the park is wilderness, which means nobody lives there except wild animals. Look carefully along the waterways. That's where most of the towns and villages are."

"Blue!" Adirondack shouted. "I found Blue! And look! There's another Blue!"

"Let me see," Kate said. She moved her finger over the place where Adirondack stood. "That's it!" she said. "Blue Mountain Lake. And Blue Mountain Lake Village is on the shore of the lake. And over there is Blue Mountain. "You did it! You solved the clue," Kate said. "Melvin must have gone to Blue Mountain Lake for some reason."

"Or Blue Mountain," Adirondack said, thinking out loud. "Although I don't know how or why he would go off like that. How would he even know how to get there?"

"That's a mystery," Kate said. "It sounds to me like somebody else had a hand in this. But at least you know where to look for him."

"Sure," Adirondack said, shaking his head. "All I'll have to do is travel across miles of endless wilderness and look for my friend while I fight off deadly wild animals and an occasional cat. Nothing to it. I'll be back with Melvin in no time."

Kate laughed. "You can hitch a ride with my dad for part of the way," she said. "He's driving to Old Forge after lunch."

Adirondack stroked his whiskers. "Do you think he'd be willing to let me come along? I mean, he didn't seem too fond of me before."

"He changed his mind after you helped rescue me on Bald Mountain," Kate said. "I'm sure he won't mind."

"Can you tell me how to get to Blue Mountain Lake from Old Forge?"

"Of course," Kate said. "I'll make a copy of the map for you. And I'll write down the number of the road you need to follow."

Adirondack handed her back the paper she had written the word Blue on. She made two new marks on the paper and handed it down to him.

"This is the number you need to look for," she said.

Adirondack studied the paper. The marks Kate had written looked like this: 28. "Where will I find this number?"

"There will be signs along the side of the road. Keep watching to make sure you are still on road number 28. And whenever you come to a place where the road divides and goes off in two directions, be sure to stay on the one marked 28."

CRASH! BANG! THUMP! The noise came from the front porch outside.

"Meow! Grow-ow-ow-l! Yowly, Yowly, Wow!"

Sammy!

Adirondack almost passed out when Kate yanked the door open.

Sammy looked at him from the back of an upside down Adirondack chair. He had a big smile on his face, and the tail of a mouse dangling from his lower lip.

CHAPTER 10

FOE OR FRIEND?

"Sammy!" Kate screamed.

"Melvin?" Adirondack cried.

Kate grabbed Sammy and shook him. "Spit that mouse out!" she yelled.

"Me-row!" Sammy said. "Pet-o-o-o!"

The mouse dropped to the porch floor. "Please don't eat me," he whimpered.

"Bad cat!" Kate said to Sammy. She opened the door and shoved him inside and shut the door behind him.

"Is that your friend?" she asked Adirondack.

"I'm not sure," Adirondack said. He moved closer. The mouse's fur was soaking wet and covered from top to bottom with gooey, drooly, sickening cat spit. He smelled awful. A lot like that fishy cat food Sammy liked to eat.

The mouse kept his paws wrapped over his head, still trying to hide. He trembled all over and made funny mewing sounds like a little baby mouse.

"I don't think that's Melvin," Adirondack said.

"Who's there?" the mouse said. "Is it safe to come out? Is that awful beast gone?"

"Rupert?" Adirondack rubbed his eyes and looked again. "What are you doing here?"

"That's none of your business, Loser," Rupert said. "Um, I mean, I wanted to help you look for Melvin." He looked over his shoulder. "You didn't happen to see where that beast went did you?" He balled his paws into fists. "I'll knock his block off if he comes back here."

"Ha, ha, ha," Kate laughed. "You weren't so brave when you were inside Sammy's mouth."

"Run!" Rupert yelled. "There's a huge giant standing right behind you!"

"That's not a giant," Adirondack said. "That's my friend, Kate."

Rupert stared up at Kate. "Too bad you can't make friends your own size," he said to Adirondack.

"You should not have followed me," Adirondack said. "I don't need your help. Go back to Seed Hollow."

Rupert made a face, like he was going to cry. "I just wanted to be your friend," he said. "I know you hate me, but I'm different now. I really want to help you find Melvin."

"You might need a friend," Kate said to Adirondack. "It's a long way to Blue Mountain Lake."

"He's not my friend," Adirondack said.

Rupert's eyes narrowed. "Did she say Blue Mountain Lake? Why are you going there?"

"To find Melvin, of course," Adirondack said.

Rupert looked nervous. He rubbed his paw over his whiskers the wrong way until they stood straight up in front of his eyes. "What makes you think you'll find him there?"

"Melvin left me a clue," Adirondack said.

"That's impossible," Rupert said.

"Why do you say that?" Adirondack said. "How would you know if he did or not?"

Rupert looked angry. "Because he's too stupid to go that far away. And you're dumber than a rock if you believe he would!" He took a step closer. "Give me that clue!"

"No," Adirondack said.

"I've seen the clue," Kate said. "Adirondack is right." Quick as a cat she picked Rupert up by the tip of his tail. She held her nose with her other hand and walked along the path that led to the back of the house.

"If you're going with Adirondack, you need a bath," she said.

"Put me down, you dumb giant," Rupert said. "Put me down. Put me down. Put me down!"

Adirondack laughed. Rupert kept yelling, 'put me down', all the way to the rain barrel near Kate's back door.

Kate held him up by his tail over the barrel. It was full of water. "You can't ride in my father's car smelling like that," she said.

Adirondack climbed up the drain pipe and sat on the edge of the rain gutter to watch.

Rupert looked down at the deep water. He trembled. All the color left his face until he looked like a brown mouse with a white face. His eyes bugged out. "Save me!" he yelled at Adirondack. "I promise I'll never be mean to you again if you save me."

"Plop!" Down into the water went Rupert. He came up, coughing and sneezing.

"Hold your breath next time," Kate said.

"Plop!" Down he went again. This time he came up with his cheeks all puffed out. As soon as he saw that he was out of the water he blew out the air and sucked in another big breath.

Kate held him close to her face and sniffed. "That's better," she said. She set him down on the ground. "I have to go talk to my father. You should dry yourself off. He won't want a wet mouse dripping all over the car seat."

CHAPTER 11

OLD FORGE

A short time later they were on their way to Old Forge. The tires on the big, black dragon hummed along the road. Of course, Adirondack knew it wasn't really a dragon, but he didn't tell Rupert that.

Adirondack pressed his face to the side window, watching trees and hills and rivers whiz by. Rupert hid inside the drink holder and made those stupid baby mouse noises.

"Your friend doesn't seem to be enjoying the ride," Kate's dad said.

He's not my friend, Adirondack wanted to say. But if he said that, Kate's dad might get mad. "He's just a little car sick," Adirondack said instead. "This is his first time."

Kate's dad smiled and nodded at Adirondack in the rear-view mirror.

"Come out of that hole and act like a big mouse," Adirondack whispered to Rupert. "We're almost there and nothing has swallowed you up yet."

Rupert crawled out of the drink holder and sat on the floor of the car. "I'll open my eyes when this thing stops roaring and moving," he said. But at least he stopped crying.

"I'll drop you off at the Old Forge Hardware," Kate's dad said. "All you'll need to do is follow the road down the hill and around a curve. When you see the Enchanted Forest, you'll know you're on the right road."

Rupert opened his eyes so wide they looked as big as the saucer Adirondack's mom set her teacup on. "What's an enchanted forest?" he whispered. His whiskers drooped. Spit dribbled from his lower lip.

"Relax," Adirondack said. "Kate says it's a place where People go to have fun."

"Is it haunted?" Rupert asked. "Full of ghosts and monsters?"

Adirondack laughed. "Well, she did say there's a big giant there. And he carries a great big ax."

Rupert shivered. "Well," he said, "if he comes after me, I'll knock his block off."

"Right," Adirondack said but he didn't believe that for a minute.

"There's Thendara Station," Kate's dad announced. He slowed the car and pulled it off the path. "Too bad we don't have time to take a ride on the train today."

"Wow!" Adirondack said. He pressed his face to the window and stared. "That's bigger than anything I've ever seen."

The wheels on this huge monster straddled a different kind of path. A path made up of big boards laying side by side in a long row. But the wheels didn't touch the boards; they perched above them on two shiny ridges.

"Take a look, Rupert," Adirondack said. "This thing is enormous! And look at all the People waiting to get on the train."

Rupert dived back into the drink holder. "I don't want to see any more People!"

Adirondack watched the train slowly roll closer to the waiting People. A whole parade of train cars followed behind the first car. "I didn't see the train last year," he told Rupert. "I must have been on the car seat inside the see-through house when we passed by."

Rupert stuck his head out of the drink holder. "I must have been in my little see-through house," he said, making his voice sound like Adirondack's.

"Copy-rat!" Adirondack whispered. He stuck his tongue out at Rupert.

Kate's dad drove the car back onto the road. "We're coming into Old Forge," he said.

"Does that mean we can get out of this death trap soon?" Rupert asked.

"What did your friend say?" Kate's dad asked.

Adirondack frowned at Rupert. "He said thank you for the ride."

Kate's dad smiled. "Glad to help," he said.

Adirondack looked out the window. People walked along the street. Here and there they walked across the path. "Look out!" he yelled, when two of them stepped off the curb in front of their car.

"That's all right," Kate's dad said. He stopped the car and waited for them to get to the other side of the street. "When People walk on the crosswalk, cars have to stop."

Adirondack pressed his nose to the window. Brightly painted stores lined both sides of the street with big glass windows filled with bright shirts and little stuffed animals – animals that he had never seen before. In another window big wooden paddles lay across a boat with a round bottom and pointy ends. Behind the boat two long, thin poles with thread hanging down from the end leaned against a fake tree. A bunch of brightly colored feathers had been tied onto the end of the thread. In front of the boat puffy pillows with green trees painted on each one lay here and there.

"Look at all this stuff," Adirondack said.

Rupert shook his head, jumped down and huddled against the car door.

Kate's dad pulled the car to the side of the path and got out. "We're here," he said. When he opened the car door, Rupert fell out onto the sidewalk.

CHAPTER 12

THIS WAY OR THAT?

Kate's dad picked Rupert up. "Your friend's a little clumsy," he said to Adirondack. He set Rupert down in front of a big building.

Rupert swayed, like he might pass out.

Adirondack jumped down from the car.

"That dumb giant tried to kill me," Rupert said.

"He's only trying to help," Adirondack said.

"You can ride back to Boonville with me," Kate's dad said. "But you'll have to meet me right here in front of the Old Forge Hardware no later than the day after tomorrow. I'll have to start back by then."

"We'll try to be here," Adirondack said.

"And I'll plan to be anywhere but here," Rupert said.

"Good luck," Kate's dad said to Adirondack. He crossed the street and disappeared in a sea of People.

"A lot of help he was," Rupert said. "What are we supposed to do now?"

"He said to follow this road around the curve and down the hill. If we see the Enchanted Forest we'll know we're on the right road."

Rupert looked astounded. "Don't tell me you plan to walk all the way to Blue Mountain Lake? There's no way you'll make it there and get back here before that dumb giant rides off on his stupid dragon."

Adirondack looked Rupert in the eye. "How do you know how long it will take to walk to Blue Mountain Lake?" he said.

"Um, I mean, everybody knows that!" Rupert said. "Didn't you learn anything in that dumb Seed Hollow Academy?"

"Well, I don't remember the teacher saying anything about Blue Mountain Lake," Adirondack said. "But we won't have any chance of getting back here in time if we don't get going." He crouched down in the starting position, like he was about to run the Cider Blaster.

"Ready, set, go!" he yelled. Adirondack's paws pounded the grassy ground beside the road. He tried not to pay any attention to the cars that whizzed by on the road.

"I'll beat you there, Pipsqueak!" Rupert yelled. But he was already panting and falling behind.

"Eat my dust, Rupert," Adirondack said. He pushed himself to run even faster.

He stopped to catch his breath and looked around. People slid down rivers of rushing water on the hill across the road. They splashed into pools filled with other laughing People.

"That must be the Enchanted Forest," Adirondack said. He took off his jacket and tied it around his middle.

Rupert flopped down on the ground beside Adirondack. His chest heaved up and down; he gulped a big breath of air. "Who cares!" he said when he could talk.

"It means we're on the right road," Adirondack said.

Adirondack picked up his knapsack and walked on.

Rupert jogged to catch up. "Where did you get the swell jacket?" he said. "Can I try it on?"

"No," Adirondack said. "My mom made it for me. I promised her I wouldn't lose it."

"I just wanted to try it on," Rupert said. He kicked at a stone. "Why do we have to walk so close to the road? Isn't there a better way? A shortcut?"

"Kate said to follow road number 28. We can't do that if we don't stay on the road."

"No wonder you're a loser," Rupert said. "We could find your dumb friend a lot faster if we cut through those trees over there." He pointed across the road.

"Melvin is not dumb," Adirondack said.

"Well, he got himself lost, didn't he?"

"Melvin didn't get himself lost," Adirondack said. "Somebody else did this to him."

"Who?" Rupert said, looking shocked. "Who would do such an awful thing?"

Adirondack looked Rupert in the eye, and then looked away. "I don't know," he said.

"So, how about trying a shortcut?"

"I don't think so." Adirondack said. He walked away.

"Wait!" Rupert yelled. "Didn't you say you had a map? Let me take a look, I'm sure I can find a better way."

"No," Adirondack said. "I'm going the way Kate said to go."

"All right. Just let me see the map."

Adirondack stopped. He pulled the map of the Adirondack Park out of his knapsack.

Rupert spread it out on the grass. "Hmmm!" he said. "See how the road twists and turns? If we went straight through the woods we could save lots of time."

"But how – "

"Come on, what are you waiting for? The faster we get started the sooner you'll find that dorky friend of yours." Rupert raced away from the road and dashed into the woods with the map.

CHAPTER 13

THE TRIP

"Wait!" Adirondack yelled. "I told you I wanted to follow the road."

"This is much better," Rupert said. "You'll love it. Just look at the beautiful scenery."

"Give me back my map," Adirondack shouted. He caught up with Rupert near a big maple tree. "Give it back," he said.

"Don't get your scarf in a tangle," Rupert said. "We don't need a map. I've got it all figured out."

Adirondack looked around. There were trees everywhere. "How do you know which way to go?"

Rupert snapped a small branch from the maple tree. He strode forward, using the twig as a walking stick. "Just follow me," he said. "We'll be there in no time."

Adirondack hurried after him. "Are you sure this is the way?"

"Of course," Rupert said. "Where do you think I traveled on my Journey? I know these woods like I know my own name."

"I had no idea," Adirondack said.

"Like that's news to anybody."

Adirondack ran to keep up, he was afraid to lose sight of Rupert. He might never find his way out of the forest alone. He jogged around rocks and fallen limbs of trees. Squirrels chattered at him from way up in the tallest branches overhead. Flies buzzed his ears. He swatted at one and missed.

Rupert kept walking. Uphill, downhill, over rocks, under mushrooms, through a small stream and around tree after tree.

"I'm getting tired," Adirondack said. "Isn't that the same twisted tree I saw where we started from?"

"Ha, ha, ha," Rupert laughed. "That's a good one. Do you think that tree is following us?"

"No," Adirondack said. "I think you don't know where you're going."

"I told you, I know these woods like I know my own name," Rupert said. He darted ahead and disappeared over the top of a hill.

Adirondack raced after him. He ran so fast that when he came over the top of the hill he couldn't stop.

Rupert waved to him from the bottom of the hill.

"Look out, Rupert!" Adirondack shouted. He waved his paws to slow himself down, but he still shot down the hill faster than a squirrel runs up a tree. Halfway down he tripped and fell. Sharp pain grabbed one back paw as he rolled the rest of the way down the hill.

Rupert ran to him. "Why don't you watch where you're going," he said. He looked at Adirondack's paw. "Ewww," he said. "I think your traveling days are over."

"I'm fine," Adirondack said. But when he tried to stand on his injured paw, he couldn't. "I just need to rest my paw for a little while."

"You're going to need lots of rest," Rupert said. He shook his head as he reached down and pulled his walking stick out from under Adirondack. "Such a shame. Poor Melvin will just have to wait a little longer."

"If you don't want to wait, just leave me the map."

"What map?"

Adirondack frowned. "My map of the Adirondack Park," he said. "The one you ran off with."

Rupert grinned. "I think I lost it somewhere. But don't worry I know where to go. I'll take care of everything." He leaned on his walking stick. "At least you didn't break my stick with your dumb fall," he said. He started back up the hill.

"Where are you going?" Adirondack called.

"Don't worry, Crybaby," Rupert said. "I won't leave you here. I've got to go back to Old Forge and find that dumb giant. I'll be back with help in no time."

Adirondack looked down at his own shadow. It had grown longer, like it always did in the late afternoon. "You'll be back before dark, won't you?"

Rupert looked down from the top of the hill. "You are not to move from that spot," he said. "If you wander off, I'll never find you." He waved his paw and then disappeared over the hill.

CHAPTER 14

MORE?

Pain pounded Adirondack's hurt paw. Tears rolled down his nose and splashed onto his jacket. "I'm so sorry, Melvin," he said. "This is going to take a little longer than I planned. But don't give up. I'll come and find you as soon as my paw feels better."

Melvin will think I'm not coming, Adirondack thought. He shook his head. What a mess I've made. My friend needed me and I failed him. And I've probably ruined my chance to be the next storyteller.

Adirondack sobbed and sobbed. He didn't stop crying until he ran out of tears. Then he closed his eyes and rested his head on some moss.

Sometime later Adirondack shook himself awake. He rubbed his eyes and looked around. Evening dew covered his jacket and winked at the fading light of the setting sun.

He jumped to his feet. "Ow!" he yelled when he stepped on his sore paw. He sat down and rubbed the hurt away. "Rupert should have come back by now," he said.

Daylight faded to shadows. "I guess I'm going to be stuck here all night, Adirondack said. "I'd better find a safe place to sleep." He picked up a broken twig and slid it under his front leg so he could lean on it. He held his hurt paw up and used the twig to swing himself forward. He searched all around the rock. He didn't dare go far for fear Rupert wouldn't see him when he came back – if he ever did come back.

"Aha!" Adirondack yelled when he spotted a log lying on the ground behind the rock. He peeked inside. The log was hollow and a pile of dry leaves inside invited him in.

Adirondack's tummy growled. He hadn't eaten anything since he left Seed Hollow. He sat down near the log and opened his knapsack. He unwrapped a big hunk of honeycomb and took a bite. Honey dripped off his chin as he sucked the sweet liquid out of the waxy comb.

"Mmmm," he said. He licked his lips and wiped his sticky whiskers with a red maple leaf. Then he rooted around in his knapsack to see what else his mom had packed. "Aha!" he said as he pulled out a piece of his mom's goldenrod seed cake. He took a big bite. "I feel better now," he said.

"Growl!"

Adirondack patted his tummy and laughed. "Be quiet," he said. "I'm eating as fast as I can."

"GROWL!"

Adirondack looked up. A huge something with long, black fur stared at him and drooled. It stood up on its hind legs and pawed the air with the biggest claws Adirondack had ever seen.

"GROWL!" it said, just like before, only louder.

Whatever this thing was it seemed to be getting mad. Adirondack trembled. He wanted to run away, but even if he didn't have a sore foot, his legs were too short to outrun something this big.

Drool dribbled off the monster's chin. That's when Adirondack noticed that it wasn't looking at him. It was eyeing his cake and honey with a longing look.

"GROWL!" it said. It dropped down on all four legs and walked closer, sniffing the air.

Adirondack threw his cake at the thing and watched it disappear into the monster's mouth. The thing stopped for a minute to sniff the dirt where the cake had been, then he walked even closer.

"Here!" Adirondack yelled. He threw his knapsack and the rest of his honeycomb at the monster and dove into the rotted log. He peeked out.

The monster slurped the honey from the piece of comb. He poked his tongue into each corner until he had licked up every last bit. Then he stuffed the waxy comb into his mouth. After he chewed and swallowed the whole comb, he smiled and licked his paws clean.

"More?" he said.

Adirondack kept quiet. He had hoped this thing would go away when the food was gone.

The monster eyed Adirondack's knapsack. He cuffed it with one huge paw. He sniffed at it with his big nose.

"Mmmm," he said. He picked the knapsack up in his teeth and shook it. Then he threw it on the ground. With one swipe of his sharp claws, he ripped it into little pieces.

"More," he said. And then he finished off the last piece of goldenrod seed cake.

The monster sat down. He burped and rubbed his tummy.

Night pulled a shade down over the last light from the setting sun. Clouds hid the moon and stars, but the monster didn't go away. His yellow eyes glowed in the darkness. He came closer, sniffing and drooling. He pushed his nose into the end of the log.

"More?" he said.

Adirondack smelled the monster's hot, honey-sweet breath. He backed away, trying not to make a sound.

The monster's tongue licked at the inside of the log. One huge paw full of razor-sharp claws grabbed the other end of the log.

Adirondack scampered to the middle. The whole log shook, so hard that he bounced from one side to the other.

"No more!" the monster shouted. "No good!" He set the log down and shoved it away.

The log rolled over and over, turning faster and faster like the wheel used to do in the see-through house Adirondack had lived in at the school. He ran as fast as he could on three paws, keeping up with the rolling log until it finally stopped.

Adirondack flopped on his back and panted. He moved his head and then his paws. Except for his sore paw nothing else hurt.

In the stillness of night an owl hooted in the distance. Bats chirped and flapped their wings as they flew above the trees. But he didn't hear the monster.

Adirondack peeked out of the log. He didn't see the monster anywhere. Fireflies danced near the rock. Adirondack crawled out of the log and limped over to what was left of his knapsack. The firefly lantern was ruined.

"We have come back to light your way," the leader of the fireflies said.

"I am thankful for that," Adirondack said in their way of speaking. "But I can't use your help this night. I am injured and I must rest. I can't leave this place."

"Are you safe here?" the firefly asked. "There is a big black bear nearby."

"I think I saw him," Adirondack said. "I hope he won't come this way again."

The firefly winked. "Shall we tell your father you are in danger?"

"You may tell my father I am safe," Adirondack said. "I will be rescued in the morning and I'll come back home soon."

The fireflies each blinked their light. "We will return when the moon awakens again," the leader said.

Adirondack watched them fly out of sight. Then he crawled inside the log and wiggled under the leaves.

Now that he was alone the forest didn't seem so quiet. Leaves rustled, twigs snapped, mosquitoes whined and beetles skittered. Adirondack stared into the darkness, afraid to close his eyes for fear the bear, or something worse, might sneak up on him if he did.

Tears ran down his cheeks when he thought about the Gathering. Soon the storyteller would choose a mouse to take his place. And here he was, stuck in the forest waiting for Rupert.

"Time is running out," Adirondack whispered to the darkness, "for me and for Melvin."

CHAPTER 15

ADIRONDACK SMELLS A RAT

Morning poured a stream of sunshine through a knothole in the log. Adirondack woke up with a start. He rubbed his eyes and limped outside.

I hope Rupert didn't come while I was sleeping, he worried. What if he left because he couldn't find me? He hurried back to the rock. But there were no fresh footprints to show that another mouse had been there. He looked up at the sky.

"It must be time for breakfast," he said. He thought about the delicious cake and honey his mom had put in his knapsack. But both were rumbling around in that bear's tummy, now.

"I'll have to find something else to eat," he said. He wandered around, searching for food. He stayed within sight of the rock though, so Rupert would see him when he came back.

Adirondack nibbled on some dried bark. Then he gnawed on the bulb of a lady slipper flower. Near the roots of a tall fir tree he found a prize – a pile of dried corn. The corn was hard to chew and tasted like sawdust, but it filled up the empty spot in his stomach. When he finished, he lapped up a few drops of morning dew from the curl of a dried leaf. Then he sat down beside the rock. The sun had moved higher in the sky.

Where is Rupert? he asked himself. He should be here by now. Unless something happened to him. Adirondack scratched his head. What if he's played a trick on me? What if he never planned to come back?

"I was a fool to believe Rupert," Adirondack said. "Look at me! Sitting here like a dumb stinkbug, waiting for that rat!"

But what else could he do? He couldn't walk very fast on his sore paw. And, thanks to Rupert, he didn't even have a map. So how would he know which way to go?

Adirondack stood up. "I have to try," he said. "Maybe I can find my way back to the road."

He tucked the twig under his front paw and limped to the bottom of the steep hill. "That hill's too high for me to climb," he said. He sat down under a bush and looked around. Then he spotted a sturdy vine growing up the trunk of a big oak tree.

Adirondack grabbed one end of the vine. He pulled himself up the vine with his front paws until he reached the other end. He yanked the vine loose from the tree and tied the smallest end into a circle. Near the circle, he tied a rock.

"I hope this works," he said. He picked up the rock and threw it as hard as he could throw. When the rock sailed up in the air, so did the vine.

"Thunk!" The rock landed halfway up the hill just above a hemlock tree. As the rock rolled back, the end of the vine got looped around the tree's trunk. When he pulled on the vine, the rock stuck tight between the tree's roots.

"Here I come, Melvin!" Adirondack yelled. He pulled himself up the vine, paw-over-paw. When he reached the hemlock tree, he tossed the rock all the way to the top of the hill. As soon as Adirondack reached the top, he set off in search of the road.

When the sun had climbed halfway to the middle of the sky, Adirondack sat down on a mossy rock. The sun warmed his back and soon he took off his coat and hung it up on a sturdy branch. He wiggled his sore paw, it hardly hurt at all. He fanned himself with a dried maple leaf.

"I'm thirsty," he said to a stinkbug. "Do you know where I can find some water?"

"What if I did?" the stinkbug said. "Why would I tell you? So you could call me dumb and make fun of me?"

"I wouldn't do that," Adirondack said.

"That's what that other bully said." The stinkbug darted under a leaf.

As soon as Adirondack lifted the leaf, the stinkbug made a beeline for another leaf.

"Wait!" Adirondack yelled. "When did you see that bully? What did he look like?"

"Leave me alone!" the stinkbug shouted. He scooted down a tiny hole and disappeared.

"Wait!" Adirondack shouted. "I promise I won't make fun of you." He dropped down on the ground beside the bug's hole. "Please come back –"

A sudden whoosh of wings made the hair stand up on Adirondack's neck. He looked up in time to see a blur of brown feathers swooping down through the trees. "E-e-e-e-e-e!" it screamed.

Only one bird screamed like that. A hawk!

Adirondack dived under some fallen leaves. He closed his eyes and waited for the hawk's sharp talons to reach under the leaves and grab him. This is the end, he thought. I'll never find Melvin, or see my mom and dad again. And I'll never be storyteller.

What's taking that hawk so long? he wondered after a few minutes. He listened. A robin chirped nearby. Adirondack peeked out. The hawk was gone, and so was his bright green coat.

"Ha, ha, ha," he laughed. "That hawk grabbed my coat instead of me." He bent down and picked up his walking stick. "I'd better get out of here before he decides to come back."

As he walked away he thought about what the stinkbug said. "Rupert must have been here," he said. "Only

Rupert would poke fun at a stinkbug."

Just look what he did to me. First, that rat tricked me into running so I would fall and hurt myself. Then he made me stay behind and wait for him. But he never went back to Old Forge to get help like he said he would. He kept going by himself. Why?

Adirondack shook his head. That didn't make any sense. Rupert didn't even like Melvin. So why would he want to rescue him?

CHAPTER 16

A CLOSE CALL

"The answers to all of my questions are waiting for me at Blue Mountain Lake," Adirondack said. "And when I get there, I'll solve this mystery."

Adirondack walked on. Fallen leaves lay like a soft rug under his paws, and over the rocks, dead twigs and branches. His injured paw hardly hurt at all anymore. Any minute now he expected to find the sign for road number 28.

After awhile the hot sun beat down from the middle of the sky. "I'm really thirsty," Adirondack said. He tried to lick his dry lips but his tongue stuck tight to the roof of his mouth. He looked around, but all he saw were dry leaves.

"Rats!" he yelled. "Stupid leaves!" He kicked at the leaves and scattered them this way and that.

Adirondack scratched his head. The leaves he had uncovered by kicking the leaves on top looked moist. He got down on his knees and carefully lifted one leaf after another. Each leaf felt wetter than the one on top of it. Inside one curled up leaf, a little pool of water gleamed in the sunlight.

"Aha!" Adirondack shouted. He didn't know how the water got in there. Maybe it trickled down from the top leaves when the last rain sprinkled the trees. Or when a heavy autumn dew wet the forest floor.

Adirondack lapped up every drop of the sweet water. It tasted delicious, like leaves, sweet mosses and tangy roots. The water cooled his throat and wet his tongue. It was the best water he had ever tasted.

All of a sudden a whir of flapping wings and a blur of feathers streaked down at him from the sky. Adirondack dived under the leaves.

"SQUAWK!"

Adirondack lifted a leaf and peeked out.

"Blue Jay?" he said. "Is it really you?"

"In the feathers," Blue Jay said. He cocked his head and winked. "Are you on your way to Bald Mountain?"

Adirondack laughed. He stood up and brushed the leaves off his fur. "I'm not here to have fun," he said. "I'm still trying to find my friend Melvin."

"Squawk!" Blue Jay said. "I think I saw him yesterday."

"Where?" Adirondack said. "Where did you see Melvin?"

"I saw him twice," Blue Jay said. "The first time he was walking north not far from here. Then a little while later

I saw him again."

"Did you say north?" Adirondack shook his head. "He shouldn't be walking away from Seed Hollow. He'll never get back home that way."

"The next time I saw him a hawk had him –"

"Oh, no!" Adirondack cried. "Poor Melvin." He covered his face and sobbed.

"Squawk!" Blue Jay said. "You didn't let me finish. I was trying to say a hawk had him on his back."

Adirondack blinked. "On his back?"

"And they were flying north." Blue Jay looked very happy with himself.

"Are you sure it was Melvin?"

Blue Jay ruffled his feathers. "Well it was a mouse." he said. He hopped up and down. "And he was wearing a bright green coat."

Adirondack's shoulders drooped. "That's my coat," he said. "I don't think that was Melvin. I'd bet my last piece of sugary baked pumpkin that was Rupert."

"You're on!" Blue Jay said. "Hop on my back. Maybe we can catch up with him and get your coat back. Will I get your last piece of pumpkin if we do?"

"Only if you fly me to Blue Mountain Lake," Adirondack said. "I need to find Melvin before Rupert does."

"What are we waiting for?" Blue Jay said.

CHAPTER 17

ARE WE THERE YET?

As soon as Adirondack climbed up onto his back, Blue Jay took off. He flew straight up through the trees. Adirondack hung on to Blue Jay's neck as tight as he could. He closed his eyes and tried not to think about what would happen to him if he let go. Up, up, and up they went. Cool air tickled his ears. As Blue Jay flew even higher, the colder air made Adirondack shiver.

After a while Blue Jay stopped climbing and they sailed along the invisible river of air. Adirondack looked down. A big blue spot of water curved along the ground below.

"What is that water?" Adirondack asked.

"People call it First Lake," Blue Jay said.

A dark winding line followed the shores of the water. "Is that the road running along the shore of the lake? And look over there. Isn't that the path to Bald Mountain?"

Blue Jay laughed. "So you do remember that's where we met," he said.

"How could I forget?" Adirondack said. "You helped me save my friend Kate there."

"And you showed me where to find those giant sunflowers," Blue Jay said. He flapped his wings and they sailed faster. "The People call this water below us now Fourth Lake," he said. "And the village there is called Eagle Bay. As soon as we turn at the end of the lake you will see the village of Inlet."

When they left Fourth Lake behind, Blue Jay flew over green trees and meadows until they reached the next big water.

"Is this Blue Mountain Lake?" Adirondack asked.

"No," Blue Jay said. "This is the lake they call Seventh."

Adirondack plucked a stray feather from his mouth. "Flying is a lot faster than walking," he said. "How much longer will it take us to fly to Blue Mountain Lake?"

"Squawk!" Blue Jay said. "I've never flown that far, but I'm sure we'll be there soon. Just keep an eye out for eagles. They get mad if you fly too close to their nest."

Adirondack looked over his shoulder. "I've never seen an eagle," he said. "What do they look like?"

"They're huge, bigger than the biggest hawk you ever saw. And if one comes after us, screaming so loud it hurts your ears, that's an eagle."

Adirondack kept looking over his shoulder, but he didn't see any huge birds. After a while he looked down again. A smaller patch of blue water winked in the sun, surrounded by green forest.

"That's the lake they call Eighth," Blue Jay said.

A little later Adirondack looked down on a long stretch of green. "Are we almost there?"

"Squawk!" Blue Jay said. "I hope so. My wings are getting tired."

"Now?" Adirondack asked a few minutes later.

Blue Jay's wings flapped slower and slower. "Not yet!"

"That must be Blue Mountain Lake!" Adirondack shouted when he saw more blue water up ahead.

"It better be," Blue Jay said. He dropped down from the sky, crashed through a tangle of tree leaves and headed straight for the water.

"Stop!" Adirondack yelled. "If I fall in the water I'll drown."

Blue Jay pulled up and landed on a thick branch.

"Where are we?" Adirondack asked.

Blue Jay's breath came in short, fast puffs. His wings drooped. "I don't know," he said. "But I can't fly another flap with you on my back. Hop onto this branch. I'll go look for something to eat and get some rest."

As soon as Adirondack slid off of Blue Jay's back, the bird flew away. Adirondack looked down. Everywhere he looked he saw water. "Wait!" he yelled at the empty sky. "Don't leave me here. I can't swim."

All of a sudden somebody or something shook the tree, so hard that the branch swayed back and forth. Adirondack hung on tight until the branch stopped shaking. Then the branch bent down toward the water.

"Help!" Adirondack yelled as the branch dipped closer and closer to the water.

CHAPTER 18

WADSWORTH

"Who's there?" a deep voice asked. "Who's on my antler? Is that you, Maggie?"

Adirondack's mouth dropped open. A talking tree? What next?

"Sure and I'll not be carrying on like that, your lordship," a tiny voice answered.

Adirondack looked, but he couldn't see anybody. "It's me," he said softly.

The branch or antler swung around. Adirondack grabbed the nearest twig and held on.

"Speak up, Sonny," the deep voice said. "These ears don't hear as well as they used to."

"Ears?" Adirondack said. "I didn't know trees had ears."

A small laugh jingled like bells. "Did you hear that, Darlin'? It thinks you're a tree."

Adirondack looked at what should have been the trunk of the tree. But instead of bark, thick brown hair covered

the place beyond his branch. And something, not far from where he sat, wiggled back and forth like a big floppy ear.

Adirondack scampered closer to the ear. "Have you seen a mouse?" he asked.

When the thing shook its head, Adirondack nearly fell off.

"I don't have a house," it said. "I live in this swamp near the shores of beautiful Raquette Lake. I don't know of any moose that lives in a house, do you, Maggie?"

Maggie sighed. "Sure and I used to live in a house. It was a darlin' sweet place. A lovely wooden house with a wee dark attic where the People almost never came."

Adirondack climbed up to the tip of the ear. "I didn't say house!" he shouted. "I said mouse."

"What are you anyway?" the moose said. He flipped his ear forward.

Adirondack hung down from it by his front paws. He stared at his own reflection in the moose's big, brown eye. "Hold still!" he yelled. "I can't swim. If I fall in this water I'll drown."

"My name's Wadsworth," the moose said. "But you can call me Worthy. I was named for Wadsworth Mountain, it's over there somewhere." He flicked his ear back and sent Adirondack flying.

"Arrgh!" Adirondack yelled. He landed on a clump of soft fur on top of the moose's head.

"Now where did that little feller go?" Wadsworth asked.

Adirondack climbed down between the moose's eyes and stood on his nose. He waved his paw. "Here I am," he said.

Wadsworth blinked. "Well, dip me in sweet tree sap and call me flapjack. It's a little, bitsy-bit of a mouse."

"Awwwww," Maggie said. "A wee little mouse."

Adirondack jumped up and down. "Why can't you hear me?" he shouted.

"You don't need to jump," Wadsworth said. "I don't have any trouble seeing, you know." Then he smiled a small smile, like he finally understood. "If you've got something to say why don't you try my other ear? That's my good ear, or at least it used to be."

Adirondack scampered up Wadsworth's nose and climbed up onto his head. When he stood on tippy toes, he could see Wadsworth's other ear, and beyond that, the other antler. And hanging down from the antler, from every single part of it, he saw a huge spider web. One thick strand of web even ran between the antler and the ear.

"Are you there yet?" Worthy asked.

Adirondack scratched his head. How could he get to that ear without getting tangled up in that web?

Maybe I can wiggle under the strand without touching it, he thought.

He studied the web. It had been carefully spun in a lovely, lacy pattern that sparkled like a fancy snowflake in the bright sunlight. The web looked beautiful, but he knew it was dangerous.

Adirondack shivered when he thought about the poor helpless fly he had once found struggling to free itself from a sticky web just like this. He wanted to help the fly get away, but as soon as he reached for the fly the web glued itself to his paw. He pulled and pulled, but his paw stayed stuck. Then a big, ugly spider ran straight for him from across the web. A burst of fear gave him the strength to jerk his paw away before the spider got him. He had been so scared he ran all the way home and hid under his bed until suppertime.

Adirondack leaned out and looked for the spider who owned this web. She must be hiding, he thought. But I'll bet she's ready to spring out and capture anything foolish enough to get stuck in her web.

"I can't hear you!" yelled the moose.

Adirondack dropped to his belly and wriggled toward the strand of web that stood between him the moose's ear. He scooted ahead until he was under the middle of the strand. Just a little farther, he told himself.

"Hmmmmm!" hummed a mosquito. "There's nothing quite as tasty as blood from a mouse's ear."

"Get away!" Adirondack yelled. He swatted at the mosquito, but his paw hit the sticky web instead.

CHAPTER 19

MAGGIE

"Faith and Begorrah!" Maggie shouted as she raced out from some hidden place and dashed across her web. She was chubby and brown, with short hairy legs and big round eyes as black as coal. She ran lightly, touching only the non-sticky spots on her web with each of her eight feet.

Adirondack struggled to free his paw from the web.

Worthy flicked his ear. He whipped Adirondack, still tangled in the piece of web, up behind his ear. "Is that you, Maggie?" he hollered. "What the Sam Hill are you doing over there?"

"Tis the wee mouse," Maggie said, sounding disappointed. "He's ripped me web."

"I'm sorry," Adirondack said. "I didn't mean to tear it. The moose told me to come over here so I could talk into his good ear. If it wasn't for that pesky mosquito, I never would have touched your web."

"Sure, and have you thought about going into the business of storytellin'?" Maggie said. "That excuse sounds like a bit of a tall tale to me. Are you sure you didn't kiss the Blarney Stone?"

Adirondack blinked back tears. "I do want to be the storyteller, more than anything," he said. "But I've never kissed a stone in my whole life, and that's the truth." Adirondack pulled at the piece of web on his paw; it stuck itself to his other paw, too.

"Well, don't get your wee whiskers in a knot," Maggie said. "Come here and let me get what's left of my lovely web off of your furry little body."

"How do I know you won't wrap me up tight and then eat me?" Adirondack said. He chewed on the web, but all that did was to twist one strand around his whisker.

Maggie's small laugh tinkled. "I'm not the type who would wrap up a mouse." she said. "Sure and that would be the mister."

"Who's the mister?" Adirondack said. He looked over his shoulder.

"Himself," she said. "The Lord of the land. King of Blarney. The big cheese." She chuckled. "Or so he thinks."

Adirondack held his breath as Maggie crawled back and forth across the thread of web that still stuck tight to his paws and his whiskers. As she went along she moistened the web with her spit. Almost immediately the web dissolved and fell away.

"Your husband," Adirondack said. "Where did you say he was?"

"Oh, I really can't say," she said. She batted her long black eyelashes. "He's a bit of a recluse, you know, always going off somewhere. I never know where or when he'll turn up again." She sighed and dabbed at her eyes with a small leaf. "A body gets used to living alone."

"What did you mean when you said he would wrap up a mouse?" Adirondack asked.

CHAPTER 20

TIME TO CLEAN THE CLOSET

"Where is that mouse?" Worthy yelled. "What's taking him so long to get to my other ear?"

"Keep your shirt on!" Maggie shouted, no louder than the whisper of the wind in the pine trees. She smiled at Adirondack. "You'd best be after doing your business, now, Dearie. That moose is getting on my nerves."

"Thank you for your help," Adirondack said. He scampered to the front of the moose's ear and leaned close to the opening. "Can you hear me now?" he asked.

"Are you there yet?" Worthy replied.

Adirondack looked closer. A bunch of dried pine needles stuck out of the ear. He pulled one out, and then he pulled out ten more. "Is that better?" he asked.

"What?" Worthy said.

Adirondack walked into the ear. He pulled out seven tiny, green pine cones, one by one. "How about now?" he shouted.

"I think I heard something," Worthy said.

Adirondack walked farther into the ear. Dried grass completely blocked the opening. Adirondack pulled out all nine blades of grass.

"Hey," Worthy said. "Who's scratching around in my ear? Hee, hee, hee. That tickles."

Adirondack pulled out five acorns. Then he took out two dried dandelion flowers. Behind the dandelions, at the very end of the ear canal, he found a tiny scrap of blue cloth. It was the same color as the piece of cloth he had found on the race track. He tugged on the cloth, but it was stuck tight to a bit of ear wax.

"Ow," Worthy said when Adirondack yanked the cloth free. "Who did that?"

"It's me, Adirondack Mouse!" Adirondack shouted. He rolled the piece of cloth up and hid it in his paw.

"No need to shout!" Worthy yelled. "I'm not deaf, you know."

Adirondack covered his mouth to keep from laughing out loud. He walked out of the moose's ear. "Can you hear me?" he asked.

"Yes!" Worthy shouted. "I hear you!"

"My stars!" Maggie cried as she ran up her newly spun thread to the moose's ear. Her black eyes looked angry. "What have you done to my wee closet? And where are all my things?"

"What closet?" Worthy asked. "Is that what you've done to my ear, Madam, stuffed it full of your junk?" He snorted. "No wonder I've been as deaf as a stone."

Maggie huffed; she dabbed at her eyes and sniffled. "Sure and I meant no harm," she said. " 'Twas such a cozy place to keep my riches."

"I said you could spin your web in my antler," Worthy said. "But if you want a home with a closet, you'll have to find another place to live."

Maggie shook all over. "Are you turning me out then? A poor old spider woman with no one to turn to and nowhere to go?"

Adirondack looked Maggie in the eye. "I don't think she'll do it again," he said.

"I swear on me poor husband's grave," Maggie said.

Adirondack frowned. "You never said your husband was dead."

Maggie pouted. "Well, he will be someday won't he?"

Worthy rubbed an itch on his neck against the bark of a tree limb that hung out over the water. "She does keep down the deer flies and mosquitoes," he said. "And it was nice to have someone to talk to, when I could hear her." He nodded his head. "All right, Maggie. Since you have promised not to use my ear for a closet anymore, you can stay." He looked up as Adirondack scampered down his nose.

"You have done me a great favor," Worthy said. "I can hear everything, now. Did you just hear that frog splash into the water? And that fish jump up to catch a buzzy fly?" A big tear hung down from his eye. "And, for the first time in a very long time I hear the beautiful song of the cardinal bird." His lips curved up in a big rubbery smile. "Would you mind having a look-see at my other ear?"

"No!" Maggie yelled. "Haven't you bothered the wee mouse enough for one day?" She ran after Adirondack as he headed for the other ear. "Tell him you're tired. Tell him you have to go now."

"I don't mind cleaning out his other ear," Adirondack said.

Maggie dashed around Adirondack and stopped between him and the ear. She looked angry and scared at the same time. "Stop!" she shouted. "Don't come any closer."

"Pay no attention to that pesky spider," Worthy said. "Take a look there. If you see any of her junk, I'll be thankful if you clean it out."

"No!" Maggie shouted. She got down on her knees – all eight of them. "Not my wee ones. I can't let you harm one hair on me babies' legs!"

"Do you mean to say you have put your children in his ear?" Adirondack said.

"Of course I didn't put my wee babes in his ear," Maggie said, looking insulted. "But it was the perfect place to store my eggs. And they have just hatched. They'll only need to stay there for a few more days. Then they'll be big enough to come out."

"Hmmm," Adirondack said. "Perhaps we can make a deal."

"Oh, I knew you were a trustworthy mouse. One that would never stoop so low as to harm a wee child."

"I'll ask the moose to let your children stay if you tell me where you got this." Adirondack unrolled the scrap of blue cloth and held it up for her to see.

CHAPTER 21

WADSWORTH MAKES A PLAN

Maggie shook so badly that her legs knocked together. "Why, 'tis only a wee gift from the mister," she said.

"Where did he get it?" Adirondack asked.

Maggie backed away. "I shouldn't say," she said. Then she stopped and looked him in the eye. "I didn't steal it. I earned it."

"Really," Adirondack said. He tapped his paw. "And what did you do to earn this cloth?"

Maggie smoothed the hair on her front legs. "Well, I don't like to brag," she said. "But I'm the best web maker there ever was." She smiled a shy smile. "I know I shouldn't say so, but it's true." She puffed out her chest and danced a few steps. "When I put me mind to it, I can spin a web strong enough to hold a bumble bee, or even a mole."

"Or a mouse?" Adirondack said.

Maggie turned pale, a sickly tan color. "I never said any such thing," she whispered.

"I don't know what this is all about," Worthy said. "But I suggest you tell the mouse everything you know about that cloth, Madam. I'd like to hear the story myself."

Maggie twisted a strand of hair on one leg. "I didn't do anything wrong," she said in a small voice. "I only did what was asked of me."

"So you spun a strong web," Adirondack said.

"Yes," Maggie said. "But I swear I didn't know what they planned to do with it."

"But now you do," Adirondack said. He held up the scrap of cloth. "My friend, Melvin, was wearing a shirt of this very color when he disappeared. I think you know what happened to him."

All the color left Maggie's face. She looked as white as a lily of the valley flower. " 'Twas the hawk," she cried. " 'Twas he who brought me the cloth. He said it was me wages for spinning the web." She covered her face with her front legs and sobbed. "I don't know anything about a mouse."

"There, there, Madam," Worthy said. "I do believe you are telling the truth, now." He lifted his head. "Come down from my ear, Mouse, and tell me about your little friend."

Adirondack slid down between the moose's eyes and stood on his nose. "I'm trying to find my friend, Melvin," he said.

"Why didn't you say so?"

"I tried," Adirondack said. "You couldn't hear me."

"Um, right." Worthy cleared his throat. "I forgot about that."

"Melvin disappeared," Adirondack said. "But he left a clue, and my friend Kate said he must be at Blue Mountain Lake, and I've been trying to get there, but Blue Jay got tired and left me here on your antler, and I can't climb down because I don't know how to swim – "

"Slow down," Worthy said. "You're making me dizzy. Let me think."

He closed his eyes tight and wrinkled up his forehead. "Hmmm," he said. His ears stood up straight. "Aha! I've got it." His ears drooped "No, that won't work. But what if . . . Yes!" He opened his eyes and winked at Adirondack. "You just make yourself comfy up there between my ears. I'll take you to see a good friend of mine. If anybody can find your little buddy, he can."

CHAPTER 22

ON THE WAY TO EAGLE LAKE

As Worthy walked out of the water, he got taller and taller. "Wow," Adirondack said. "I had no idea you were this big."

"You just hang on, Sonny," Worthy said as he trotted toward the road. "We've got to get a-going if we want to reach Eagle Nest before dark."

"Wait," Adirondack said. "Isn't it dangerous to get too close to an eagle's nest?"

Worthy snorted. "Eagle Nest is not an eagle's nest. It's a place; a very nice place near Eagle Lake."

"But there must be eagles there," Adirondack said. The thought of being ripped apart by an angry eagle sent a shiver up his back.

When he reached the road, Worthy walked to the middle and stopped. "Now what's all this fuss about eagles?" he asked.

"Well —"

"Look out!" Maggie screamed.

"Honk! Honk!" said a big red dragon, um, truck as it screeched to a stop. The driver shook his fist at Wadsworth. "Get back in the woods where you belong."

"Beep! Beep!" said a black car as it swerved around Wadsworth and roared away.

Adirondack held tight to the tuft of hair between Worthy's ears, expecting the next car to crash into the moose and kill them all. "Let's get out of here," he said.

Worthy stood his ground. He looked down on the cars. "Road hogs!" he said. "They need someone to teach them how to share."

"Get off the road," another driver yelled. He skidded his yellow car to a stop on the side of the road. The big green truck behind that car headed straight for them.

"Get off the bloody road," Maggie yelled. "If you cause harm to me babes, I swear I'll never forgive you."

"Very well, Madam," Wadsworth said. "I was just trying to teach these rude People some manners."

He ran off the road. He jogged between trees and trotted around huge rocks. He ran uphill, downhill, across some creeks and splashed through small streams. Nothing slowed him down.

Adirondack bumped along on the top of the moose's head. "Aren't you getting tired?" he asked Worthy after a while.

"I'm a moose on a mission," Worthy said. "I never get tired when I have important work to do."

"Are we there yet?" Maggie said. "I don't feel so well."

"Well, don't toss your cookies on my antler," Worthy said. "I'll get us there by dark."

The sun slowly slid lower in the sky. The shadows cast by the moose and the mouse grew longer as they traveled along the shores of another blue water.

"Is this Eagle Lake?" Adirondack asked.

"Utowana," Worthy replied.

Adirondack frowned. "Yes. I do want to know," he said.

Worthy threw back his head and laughed.

Adirondack fell over backwards and rolled down to the moose's back.

"That's Utowana Lake," Worthy said when he stopped laughing.

"That's a strange word," Adirondack said as he climbed back up to the moose's head.

"They say it's a word spoken by the First People," Worthy said. "A lot of their words are still used around these parts."

"Who were the First People?" Adirondack asked.

"Well, I don't rightly know," Worthy said. "But I do know they lived here long before I was born. My father said they lived near the big waters. He said they hunted and fished when they were hungry, but they treated the land and the animals with respect and honor." He snorted. "Not like those selfish road hogs."

"Are the First People still here?" Adirondack asked as the moose rounded the tip of Utowana Lake.

"I don't know of any," Worthy said. "My father told me they went away when the other People came."

"Are we there yet?" Maggie said. "Me poor bones can't take much more of this bouncing."

Adirondack peered ahead through the thickening shadows. "Is that Eagle Lake up ahead?" he asked.

"Indeed it is," Worthy said. He walked away from the road and splashed into the shallow water between the two lakes. "It's getting too dark to travel any farther today. We'll sleep here and when morning comes, we'll look for Sagamore."

Adirondack yawned. He fluffed the hair on the top of Worthy's head to make a bed for himself. By the time he finished the sun had disappeared behind the trees. The first star of evening winked as the faint light of the moon spread across the water.

"He's mad," Maggie whispered in Adirondack's ear. "He's lost his blooming mind. Sagamore isn't here; it's back there not far from where we started."

"Are you sure?" Adirondack said.

"Of course I'm sure," Maggie said. "They call it Great Camp Sagamore. My own dear mother used to work for the rich People there." Maggie hopped up and down. "We have to make him go back."

Worthy drew in a long, loud, deep breath. When he blew it out, his lips hung down and flapped like a bull frog's throat did in the spring. He gave a snort and then did it again, only louder.

"You'll have to tell him in the morning," Adirondack said.

Another long night, Adirondack thought. He brushed a tear from his eye. Even if he started for home right now, he might not get there in time for the storytelling. And who knew what other problems he might run into. One thing was for sure. In the morning Worthy and Maggie would head back to Raquette Lake. Should he go with them? Or try to find Blue Mountain Lake alone?

CHAPTER 23

SAGAMORE

Adirondack dried his tears. When he opened his eyes, he thought the stars had come down from the sky. They winked and blinked at him from the moose's antler. Then one of the stars flew up and hung in the air right in front of his face.

Adirondack smiled. They're not stars. They're fireflies.

The leader of the fireflies landed on the moose's ear. "We have come to light your way home, Adirondack," he said.

"I'm so glad to see you," Adirondack said. "But be very careful not to go near the other antler. There's a sticky spider web there."

The leader winked his light at the others , "Thank you for the warning," he said. "Are you well?"

"Oh, yes," Adirondack said. "But I can't travel tonight. I must wait here until morning. What news do you bring?"

"Your mother and father pray for your safe return," the firefly said. "They worry and they wait."

"Tell them I will come home as soon as I rescue Melvin," Adirondack said. He looked the firefly in the eye. "What do you know of the storyteller?"

"He is an old mouse," the firefly said. "Except for that, I don't know anything."

Adirondack smiled to hide his disappointment. "You may return to your homes," he said. "I will look for you when the moon awakens again."

Adirondack watched the fireflies fly away. When he could no longer see their lights, he curled up on Worthy's head and went to sleep.

Morning dawned with a splash of bright sunlight across a pink sky. A gray mist rose up from the water and swirled around them.

As soon as Wadsworth shook himself awake, Maggie ran up his ear. "You have to turn around, you big goose!" she said. "You're going the wrong way to find Sagamore."

"I'll do no such thing, Madam," Worthy said. "Sagamore will be here any minute, and in case you haven't noticed I'm a moose, not a goose."

"Turn around!" Maggie said. "Turn around, or I swear I'll dance on your grave under a black moon if you refuse."

"There he is now," Worthy said. He pointed his nose at a tiny black speck high up in the sky. "My buddy, Sagamore Eagle. He'll come down as soon as he finds his breakfast."

"He?" Maggie said in a tiny voice.

"Eagle?" Adirondack said. He shivered.

"Imagine that," Worthy said. "Let's see: Eagle nest; Eagle Lake; Eagle! Bald Eagle in fact. Makes perfect sense to me." He puffed out his chest and rolled his eyes at Maggie. "And you, Madam, owe me an apology. And while you're at it, perhaps you'll explain why you want to dance on my grave when I'm not even gone yet?"

Maggie pouted. "It's not my fault that you never said he was an eagle. How was I to know?" She ran down from his ear and hopped onto her web. "We'll just forget the whole thing, won't we?" she said as she trotted out of sight.

Adirondack looked up. The eagle dived down from the sky feet first, headed straight for them.

Adirondack ran back and forth on the moose's head, but he couldn't find anyplace to hide. "Save me, Worthy!" he yelled. "I don't want to be eagle-breakfast."

Wadsworth tipped his head back and laughed. "I don't mean to insult you, little feller," he said. "But you're not even big enough to be breakfast for a crow."

Adirondack ducked as a blur of brown and white feathers zipped past him and splashed down into the water. Before Adirondack had time to blink, the huge bird flew back up in the air with a big fish held tight in his talons. He landed near the top of a tall fir tree.

"Sagamore will come down to visit after breakfast," Worthy said. He lowered his head and grabbed a mouthful of marsh grass. "Try some of this grass," he said. "It's mighty sweet and tender."

Adirondack leaned down and pulled a piece of grass out from between the moose's teeth. When he chewed it, the grass did taste sweet. Maybe not as sweet as sugary baked pumpkin, but sweet just the same. And just a few bites of the thick grass quieted the growl in his empty tummy.

The eagle looked down from his perch on the tree. "Is that you, Wadsworth?" he called. "I'm so very glad to see you. It's been too many seasons since you last came this way." With one mighty flap of his wings he flew down from the fir tree and landed on the limb of a maple tree that hung over the water near Wadsworth's head.

Worthy grinned. "You're a sight for moose eyes, Sagamore," he said.

Adirondack stared at the eagle. He saw danger in the eagle's big curved beak and sharp talons, and in the large, all-seeing eyes that stared back at him.

"Is this mouse your friend, Wadsworth?" the eagle asked. "Are you sure you can trust him to do the right thing?" He fixed Adirondack with a look of distrust.

"Silly me," Worthy said. "I plumb forgot my manners, Sagamore." He nodded his head. "This here mouse goes by the name of Adirondack. He has been a true friend to me. And over there on my antler is my little spider-buddy, Maggie."

Sagamore turned a sharp eye on Maggie. "That one bears watching," he said. "Spiders can't always be trusted to do the right thing."

Maggie backed into her hiding place without a word.

"You might be right about that," Worthy said. "When I wasn't looking she turned my ear into her closet and stuffed it so full I couldn't hear a thing. Adirondack, here, cleared it out for me." He nodded his head. "In fact that's why I came here to find you. Adirondack needs your help."

When the eagle turned back to him, Adirondack wanted to run and hide. But if anyone could find Melvin, Sagamore could. So he lifted his chin and stood tall.

"I'm trying to find my friend, Melvin," he said in a small voice. "Have you seen him?"

Sagamore preened a wing feather. "I see everything: the mountains; the trees; the water; and every creature that flies, walks or swims here. I see many mice. How would I know which one is your friend?"

Adirondack's hope surged. "He's little and brown like me, and I think he's somewhere near Blue Mountain Lake, and he might be wearing a blue shirt."

Sagamore blinked. "Would he be in the company of a mouse in a bright green jacket?"

"That's my jacket!" Adirondack cried.

"And two shady characters who have been known to be up to no good before?"

"Is one of them a hawk?" Adirondack asked.

"Yes," Sagamore said. "And the other a spider. Do you know them?"

Adirondack shook his head. "No, but Blue Jay said he saw a hawk near the place where Melvin disappeared." He frowned. "And it was a hawk that stole my jacket." He looked Sagamore in the eye. "Is Melvin all right? Where is he?"

CHAPTER 24

TO THE RESCUE

"The mouse you seek is on a small island in Blue Mountain Lake," Sagamore said. He flew down and landed on Wadsworth's antler. "I can take you there."

Doubt and fear made Adirondack hesitate. The eagle could fly even higher than Blue Jay, and Adirondack had trouble enough staying on Blue Jay's back. What if he fell off the eagle when he was flying so high above the clouds? He closed his eyes and saw himself falling and screaming and falling and screaming and . . .

"Don't be afraid," Worthy said. "Sagamore will see that no harm comes to you. You can put your trust in him." He pulled his lips up in his rubbery smile. "Did I ever tell you how Sagamore got his name?"

Adirondack shook his head.

"A wrinkled old man found this eagle when he was still a nestling," Worthy said. "He found him on a cliff near the peak of Blue Mountain where he had fallen from his nest. The old man stayed with the eagle. When the eagle's mother didn't come back, the man looked after him and brought him food until he was big enough to fly and take care of himself. It was this man who gave him the name, Sagamore. He said it was a name of honor among his People, a name given only to a chief or a very wise man. He said this name would make Sagamore honest and strong. And when Sagamore grew up he could be the protector of truth and justice; the guardian of the Adirondack Mountains and all who come here."

"Wow!" Adirondack said. He looked up at Sagamore. "My mom named me for the mountains so I would be strong and brave." He took a deep breath. "I will be honored to fly with you."

The corners of Sagamore's beak turned up, like he was smiling. "Climb aboard," he said.

"There's just one problem," Adirondack said, still worried about falling off.

"So you'll be off, then," Maggie said. "Leaving your dearest friends behind without so much as a backward glance, or even a cheery 'fare thee well'." She swung down from the antler on a single silky thread and landed beside Adirondack.

"I'm sorry," Adirondack said. "I have to go and find my friend."

"I know, Dearie," Maggie said. She dabbed at the tears in her eyes with one foot. Then she smiled. "I've made you a wee gift to remember me by."

Adirondack stepped back when he saw the loop of web curled over her back. "You're not going to trap me are you?" he said.

Maggie laughed. " 'Tis not a trap," she said. "I made these reins for you from my best non-stick thread. You can put them around Mr. High and Mighty's neck, over there." She bowed to the eagle. "That way you'll have something to hang onto as you fly away with my heart."

"That's most kind – Maggie, isn't it?" Sagamore said. He fixed her with a stare. "What do you know about this spider on the island at Blue Mountain Lake?"

Maggie handed the web-reins to Adirondack and sighed. "I'll be asking you to remember my kindness to this mouse when you meet my poor husband, your lordship," she said. "He's not a bad sort, he's only been tricked by that hawk. I beg you to treat him with kindness and send him home to his lonely wife and wee babies."

"I will remember what you have done for this mouse," Sagamore said. He stretched his wing down so that it touched the antler.

Adirondack walked up Sagamore's wing to his back. He wrapped the web-reins around Sagamore's neck twice and then curled the two ends around his front paws before he sat down. He looked down at Wadsworth and Maggie.

"I'll never forget what the two of you have done for me," Adirondack said. "I hope we will meet again another day."

"You be careful, little feller," Worthy said. A big tear hung down from his eye.

"The luck of the Irish be with you," Maggie said. "And a big fat curse on that hawk."

Adirondack laughed. "Goodbye!" he called.

Sagamore flapped his strong wings and the two of them rose up in the air.

Adirondack squeezed his eyes shut, gritted his teeth and hung on tight to the reins. Cool, cold, and then colder air rushed past him as Sagamore climbed higher and higher. Except for the warmth from the eagle's body, I'd be frozen solid by now, Adirondack thought.

When Sagamore finally stopped climbing, they sailed out on an ocean of air. Adirondack opened his eyes and looked down between fluffy white clouds. He rubbed his eyes and looked again. He couldn't see any trees or lakes or rivers. There were only squares of color: dark green where the forest should have been; a scrap of lighter green here and there for the fields; silver threads of river; and splashes of blue lakes.

"Wow!" Adirondack said. "Everything looks different from way up here."

"I fly high in the sky so I can see a great distance," Sagamore said. "It's my job to watch over the whole Adirondack Park."

All I can see are squares of color," Adirondack said.

"Ah," Sagamore said. "That's because you are looking through the eyes of a mouse. If you could see with the eyes of an eagle you would see everything, just like I do." Sagamore lifted his wings to slow them down. "Do you see that spot of blue way down there under my wing? That's Blue Mountain Lake. And that tiny dot of green on the blue? That's the island where your friend is trapped."

Adirondack peered down through the clouds. "I only see the blue color," he said.

"I'll fly down closer, but we have to be careful. We don't want the bad ones to see us until we have a plan."

Adirondack held tight to the reins as they dropped under the clouds and then down, down, down from the sky.

Sagamore landed on the ledge of a tall building near the lake. "This is the Adirondack Museum," he said. "The People here collect and keep the history of their life in the mountains. And this ledge is a great look-out post." He pointed with his beak. "Do you see the island now?"

"Yes," Adirondack said. "But I can't see Melvin."

"I saw Melvin and the others as we flew down," Sagamore said. "They made their camp near the skinny pine tree at this end of the island. The hawk and the mouse wearing the green jacket appear to be arguing. The spider has spun his web on the lowest branch of the tree. Melvin is sitting on a rock behind them." He turned to Adirondack. "What do you wish to do?"

Adirondack rubbed his whiskers. "If you can scare them, I will try to get Melvin away from them."

Sagamore smiled. "That will not only be easy, it will be fun. I can't wait to see the looks on their faces when they see me coming."

A few minutes later, Sagamore circled the island with Adirondack on his back. Adirondack saw the pine tree, now, and what looked like a tiny mouse. One mouse ran after a hawk. Behind them, another mouse sat on a rock.

"Hang on!" Sagamore yelled. "We're going down!"

Adirondack held tight to the reins and gritted his teeth as he and the eagle dropped into a steep dive.

"Kleek – kik – ik – ik – ik!" Sagamore screamed.

CHAPTER 25

THIS EAGLE IS MY FRIEND

Adirondack opened his eyes. As he and Sagamore fell from the sky the rush of air tugged at him and tried to pull him off the eagle's back. Any minute he expected to fall to the ground. He locked his knees around the feathers on Sagamore's back and leaned closer to the eagle's neck. Sagamore's angry screams raised goose bumps all over Adirondack's body.

"Kleek – kik – ik – ik – ik!" Sagamore screamed again and again.

Adirondack looked down. Rupert ran around the pine tree. He shook his fist at the hawk as it flew away. The spider's web looked empty. Melvin ducked behind the rock.

"Get ready, Adirondack," Sagamore said as his feet touched the ground.

Adirondack slid off the eagle's back and raced for the rock where Melvin was hiding. But when he ran past the pine tree, Rupert jumped out at him.

"Adirondack," Rupert said. "I knew you'd come to rescue me. I was taken prisoner by a big ugly hawk and a mean-as-dirt spider. They brought me here and they won't let me go." He grabbed Adirondack's shoulders. "You have to save me!"

At first Adirondack didn't know what to do. What if Rupert was telling the truth? After all, Blue Jay did say he saw Rupert flying north with a hawk. But Blue Jay also said that Rupert was riding on the hawk's back, not caught in his talons.

"Get out of my way!" Adirondack said. But Rupert wouldn't let go of him.

"I said you have to save me," Rupert said. "Now tell that overgrown bird over there that I'm your friend." He shook his fist. "And when I catch up with that hawk and his eight-legged pal I'll knock both their blocks clean off."

Adirondack pushed Rupert away, so hard that Rupert landed on his bottom. Then he yanked his green jacket off of Rupert and ran away with it.

"Hey!" Rupert yelled. "You come back here!"

Adirondack raced for the rock. "Melvin!" he shouted. "It's me, Adirondack."

Melvin peeked over the rock. His eyes got as big as dinner plates. "Look out, Adirondack!" he yelled. "There's a huge bird coming after you." He dived down behind the rock.

109

Adirondack looked over his shoulder. Sagamore hopped toward them on one foot. With his other foot he held Rupert tight.

"I'll keep this mouse out of trouble until you and your friend are ready to fly away," he said.

Rupert stuck his tongue out at Adirondack. But he didn't dare say a word.

"Come on out, Melvin," Adirondack said. "This eagle is my friend."

Melvin peeked over the rock. "Are you sure?"

Adirondack ran behind the rock and hugged Melvin. "I was so afraid something awful had happened to you," he said. "Afraid I'd be too late to rescue you."

"You almost were," Melvin said. "I heard Rupert and the others talking last night. They planned to leave me here alone tomorrow. Rupert said it was a pity I can't swim. He said I might live for a week or two with no food, but not much longer."

"That rat!" Adirondack said. "But look who's caught now." He pointed at Rupert, still wrapped tight in the eagle's talons.

CHAPTER 26

MELVIN'S STORY

"You come back here!" Rupert yelled.

Adirondack looked down as Sagamore flew up in the sky, higher and higher. Rupert shook his fist. He already looked smaller.

"Kleek!" Sagamore screamed. "I'll come back for you later."

Itsy bitsy Rupert threw himself down and beat his tiny fists on the ground. Adirondack and Melvin laughed.

"Hang on to my jacket," Adirondack said to Melvin. "Once Sagamore gets high enough, the ride will get easier."

"I hope so," Melvin said. He pressed his face against Adirondack's back and held on tighter. "You should have seen Rupert carry on when the hawk came back with this jacket instead of you. He was so mad he held his breath until his face turned purple."

"Ha, ha, ha," Adirondack laughed. "I'm glad I got my jacket back. I promised my mom I wouldn't lose it."

Sagamore stopped flapping his wings and held them out straight. He sailed across the ocean of air high above Blue Mountain.

"Wow!" Melvin said. "Sagamore flies higher than the hawk. And I can enjoy the view this time, since I'm not hanging upside down from sharp talons."

Adirondack looked down. Snow capped the peak of Blue Mountain and misty clouds circled the sharp rocky slopes.

I will never forget the beauty of that great mountain, he thought. Or the joy I felt when I found Melvin.

"Tell me what happened to you?" he asked Melvin. "I heard you were running the Cider Blaster, but the next thing I knew you disappeared."

Melvin sighed. "That seems like a long time ago. I ran even faster than last year at the start of the race. I ran so far ahead of the others that I couldn't hear them running behind me. Then all of a sudden I ran into a huge, spider web. It stuck to me like glue and wrapped around me." He shivered. "When I fell down, somebody or something pushed me off the track. Leaves stuck to the web as I rolled down the hill. By the time I stopped I couldn't see a thing."

"How awful," Adirondack said. "Did you tear your shirt when you fell?"

"Maybe," Melvin said. "I think I backed into a tree branch when I tried to get out of the web."

"I found a piece of your shirt," Adirondack said. "That's how I knew you had been there."

"Then that branch did me a real favor," Melvin said.

"What happened next?" Sagamore said. "This is a most interesting story."

"At the time it was more like a bad dream," Melvin said. He took a deep breath. "A spider jumped on me. The leaves crackled and rustled as he crawled all over me. I thought for sure he was going to eat me up. But the next thing I knew the spider web fell right off me."

"Why didn't you run away when you got loose?" Adirondack asked.

"Well," Melvin said. "When the web came off, I found myself face-to-face with a mean-looking hawk and a nasty spider. When they told me you were in great trouble, I forgot all about running away."

"They lied," Adirondack said. "I was at the Gathering, looking for you."

"They told me you were lost on an island in Blue Mountain Lake," Melvin said. "They said if I didn't help you, you would die. That's why I went with them."

"I would have gone, too," Adirondack said.

Sagamore nodded his head. "Friends should help their friends," he said.

"I had to try to find you," Melvin said. "But I didn't trust those two, so I left a clue in the dirt – did you find it?"

"Yes!" Adirondack shouted. "That's how I knew

where to look for you." He scratched his whiskers. "But how did you know how to make that word?"

"When I made my Journey I found a huge stone building in the People's village," Melvin said. "They called it a library. They must have liked that library a lot because they gave it a name: Erwin. I made my home there until the next Planting Season. Erwin the Library is full of books and each book is filled with strange markings. Every day, after the People went home, I studied those markings and tried to figure them out. Then, one day I finally found a book that I could understand. I was so excited I raced all around the library shouting, 'I got it!' to every single book."

"Why could you read that book and not the others?" Adirondack asked.

"Because the pictures showed me what the marks said. It's a wonderful book; I read it over and over, so many times I know the first page by heart."

"Tell it to me," Adirondack begged.

"One fish, two fish, red fish, blue fish," Melvin recited. "If you could see the colorful pictures in that book, you would see that the People's words sound exactly the same as ours." He sighed. "That's how I knew how to write the word for blue. I'm not sure I spelled it right, but I hoped that whoever saw it could figure it out."

"I didn't know what the word said. But I had seen People's writing at the school where I made my home during my Journey. So I took it to my school-friend Kate, she helped me figure it out."

"It's funny when you think about it," Melvin said. "I risked my life to save you, and all that time you were trying to find me." He gave Adirondack a squeeze. "Thank you."

"We're almost in Old Forge," Sagamore said. "Are you sure you don't want me to take you all the way to Seed Hollow?"

"I promised to meet Kate's father in Old Forge," Adirondack said. "He'll be waiting for me there."

The sun had sunk low in the sky. I hope Kate's dad didn't start for home without me, he thought.

CHAPTER 27

OLD FORGE HARDWARE

Sagamore landed on the doorstep of the Old Forge Hardware store. Adirondack and Melvin slid down the bird's open wing.

"I don't see his car anywhere," Adirondack said. His last hope fell to the bottom of his stomach.

"Maybe he's inside the building waiting for you," Melvin said.

Just then the door swung open and a man walked out. "Come on!" Adirondack said.

By the time the door swung shut, Adirondack and Melvin were both inside the store. Adirondack looked around. The store was divided into long strips with shelves on either side of each strip. Every shelf swelled with things for People to buy.

Adirondack's stomach tied itself into a big worry-knot. "We'll have to look up and down every one of these strips," he said. "That will take a very long time."

"If we split up, each one of us looking at a different strip, it will be faster," Melvin said.

"Good idea!" Adirondack dashed down the first strip, then up another.

"He's not here," Adirondack said when they finally met at the end of the last strip.

Melvin pointed to a ramp. "Maybe he's up there."

They raced up the ramp and then ran up and down, searching. Shelves held piles of bright, colorful things, and at the ends of each row of shelves, racks burst with books of every size and shape.

"Look!" Melvin said. He climbed up one metal rack and pointed to the cover of a book. "It's 'One Fish, Two Fish, Red Fish, Blue Fish'!"

People's shoes thundered on the floor. "Don't move," Adirondack whispered. "Maybe they won't see us." He dived under a nearby shelf. When he peeked out from his hiding place, he almost giggled.

Melvin stood as still as a statue with his cheeks puffed out with air and a big fat grin on his face. He looked a lot like the toy mouse on the shelf behind him.

A lady with a pencil behind her ear came around the corner. Her eyes fell on Melvin. "What's this?" she said. "I don't remember putting a stuffed mouse by that book." She reached for Melvin.

Melvin's grin disappeared. And then so did he. He blew out his breath, passed out and fell off the rack.

By **Dr. Seuss**

 **One fish**

 **two fish**

red fish

 **blue fish**

Adirondack rushed forward and caught Melvin before he hit the floor.

The lady's eyes got big. "Real mice?" she said.

Adirondack closed his eyes and waited for the ear-splitting scream. When it didn't come, he looked to see what she was up to.

The lady bent down. "Is one of you Adirondack?"

Adirondack fanned Melvin's face with one paw. He wanted to run away, but he couldn't leave Melvin alone with her.

If I don't talk to her she might go away, he thought. After a few minutes he looked over his shoulder to see if she had gone.

The lady smiled at him. "Cat got your tongue?"

"That's not funny," Adirondack said. He quickly put his paw over his mouth. Why did he talk ? Now she would never go away.

Melvin opened his eyes. "Did somebody say cat?"

"She's just playing a trick on us," Adirondack said.

The woman tapped her foot and raised one eyebrow.

Adirondack shrugged his shoulders. She didn't look like she was going to go away. He might as well ask her about Kate's father.

"I'm looking for a man," Adirondack said. "He drives a black car."

Melvin's eyes got big when he looked up at the lady. "Let's get out of here, Adirondack," he said.

"Aha," the lady said. "You are Adirondack Mouse. I've been waiting for you. The man you're looking for asked me to tell you he couldn't wait any longer. He asked me to call him if you didn't have any other way to get home. He said he could come back for you tomorrow."

Adirondack groaned. "Tomorrow will be too late." His words repeated over and over inside his head, Too late! Too late! Too late!

"Sagamore can take us home," Melvin said.

"Great idea," Adirondack said. "I'll go find him." As he hurried away he heard the woman say to Melvin, "Do you like that book?"

"Sagamore?" Adirondack called as he burst out the door.

The eagle flew down to the step. "You were gone so long I thought you had found your friend's father," he said. "I was just about to look for a tall evergreen tree and bed down for the night."

120

"Night?" Adirondack looked around. Beyond the circle of light from the streetlight, the dark of night covered everything.

Adirondack sat down hard on the step. He swallowed the lump in his throat and swiped his paw at the tears that stung his eyes. "Then it's over," he said. "I ran a good race, but I lost." He hit the step with his fist. "Rupert was right! I am a loser!"

CHAPTER 28

IT IS ALL RIGHT

"What have you lost?" Sagamore said. "A little time, nothing more."

"You don't understand," Adirondack said. "Tonight the storyteller will choose another mouse to be the next storyteller for the whole clan of the field mice. It's what I've always wanted. But by the time I get home it will be too late."

"Well, that still doesn't make you a loser," Sagamore said. "Wasn't there something else you wanted to do?"

"No," Adirondack said. "At least not until Melvin disappeared."

"And didn't you know that you might not find Melvin in time? Didn't you know that you might never find him? Did you really expect to get back in time for the storytelling?"

"Oh, I knew I might not make it," Adirondack said. "The important thing was to find my friend. That was the right thing to do!"

"You don't sound like a loser to me," Sagamore said. "You did find Melvin, and saved his life as well."

Adirondack sighed. "I will have some exciting stories to tell when I get home, even if I only get to tell them to my grand-mice someday."

"Hey, Adirondack," Melvin called from the doorway. "Come here and help me with my book."

The lady stood behind Melvin holding the very book that Melvin had learned to read. When she handed it down, Adirondack grabbed one end and Melvin took hold of the other.

"Should I tell your friend's father you'll need a ride home tomorrow?" she asked.

"Kleek!" Sagamore said.

"Oh, my," the lady said. "Look at the beautiful bald eagle."

"That's Sagamore," Adirondack said. "With his help we'll be home before noon tomorrow."

"Sagamore," she said. "A noble name for such an important bird. Did he tell you that he's the symbol of the strength and freedom of The United States of America?"

"What's that?" Adirondack asked.

"The whole country of our people," she said. "I'm sure Sagamore will bring you home safely."

A short time later, Adirondack and Melvin curled up together on a tuft of pine needles under Sagamore's wing. Adirondack pulled his green jacket up over them like a blanket. Melvin's book leaned against a nearby branch. The fireflies danced around them, blinking their lights happily.

"I can't wait to get home," Melvin said. "Do you think we'll be there in time for the storytelling?"

Melvin's question got caught in Adirondack's throat for just a minute. "No," he said. "The storytelling was going to take place tonight."

"I'm sorry." Melvin patted Adirondack's paw.

"It's all right," Adirondack said, and to his surprise it really was all right. "I could have chosen to stay home. But being storyteller wouldn't make me happy if you weren't here with me, my friend."

Melvin gave Adirondack a big hug. "We can tell our stories to each other," he said. "After all, that's what best friends are for!"

Adirondack's heart filled with joy. "I couldn't agree more," he said.

CHAPTER 29

COMING HOME

Early the next morning, before the sun had time to dry the dewy grass, Sagamore soared high in the sky with Adirondack and Melvin on his back. Soon they sailed the ocean of air, floating and riding the waves above the clouds.

"Do you want me to bring you to your home in Seed Hollow?" Sagamore asked.

"I don't know," Adirondack said. He turned to Melvin, who had one arm clamped around Adirondack's waist and the other hand holding tight to his book. "Do you think everyone left the Gathering last night or will they still be there?"

"Let's land at the Gathering. There's bound to be some mice still there. Maybe we'll get to meet the new storyteller."

"Right," Adirondack said. "I wonder who he chose."

"Well, one things for sure," Melvin said. "It can't be Rupert."

125

"Ha, ha, ha," Adirondack laughed. "He's probably still running around that island on Blue Mountain Lake and waiting for us to come back."

"I don't think so," Sagamore said. "Look down there." He dipped one wing and pointed.

"Whoa!" Adirondack shouted. He grabbed the web-reins with both paws and held on tight until Sagamore raised his wing again. Then he looked down. He blinked his eyes and looked again.

"Rupert! It's Rupert riding on a hawk!"

"I should have given that hawk a talking to," Sagamore said. "I should have told him to stay away from that mouse.

"They're making good time," Melvin said. "They must have flown all night. At this rate they may get back to the Gathering before us."

Rupert looked up at them. He shook his fist and shouted something but the wind whipped his words away before Adirondack could hear them. The hawk looked up too. Didn't he see that he was headed straight for a big puffy cloud?

"Look out!" Adirondack yelled.

The hawk shot into the cloud at full speed. A few seconds later the cloud spit Rupert and the hawk out its other end. The hawk's feathers looked all ruffled and wet; Rupert's whiskers drooped with a heavy cloud-moustache which matched his puffy white eyebrows.

"Ha, ha, ha," Adirondack laughed. But he watched them get smaller as they raced away toward home and he stopped laughing.

"Don't worry," Sagamore said. "That hawk will wear himself out long before he reaches Park Hill." He raised his beak to the sun. "I will get you there well ahead of any hawk."

"We don't have to hurry," Adirondack said. "The storyteller has made his choice so it doesn't matter if Rupert gets home first." He turned back to Melvin. I'll bet my mom will cook us a delicious feast when we get there," he said. "And after dinner we'll have the rest of the day to tell Mom and Dad all about your mysterious disappearance."

"Going down!" Sagamore shouted a few minutes later.

The wind whipped past Adirondack and Melvin as they fell from the sky in a steep dive. At first Adirondack kept his eyes shut. But the wind lost some of its strength as they came closer to the ground and he so wanted to see Park Hill again.

"Look!" he shouted to Melvin. "There's something going on at the Gathering!"

"Yeah," Melvin said. "They're running for cover. They think an eagle is coming after them."

Adirondack laughed. "Well, in a few minutes they'll know this eagle is our friend."

They circled the very top of Park Hill. An old

mouse stood alone there. A very old mouse with grey whiskers in a long red cape. In his hand he held his walking stick. He looked up at them and pointed. He waved his hand in welcome as they landed. And, although he couldn't be sure, Adirondack thought he saw the old mouse smile.